The Legend of the Emerald Lady

Nancy stayed awake, thinking about the events at Sugar Moon. Except for the whirring of the ceiling fan and the rustling of the breeze through the banana tree outside, the house was dead silent.

Nancy sat up. Was it her imagination or were there footsteps creaking across the attic floor above her?

Nancy threw off the covers and crept down the dark hall toward the circular staircase to the attic. Holding her breath, Nancy climbed the old stairs. Her heart pounded with each step that let out a horrible creak.

The footsteps in the attic grew louder. Nancy peered inside. Nothing stirred in the room. As far as Nancy could see, it was completely empty except for the litter on the floor. Could the person have heard her and left? she wondered. Nancy stepped inside.

Then something grabbed her from behind. Before she had a chance to scream, a hand clamped over her mouth.

Nancy Drew
Mystery Stories

#104 The Mystery of the Jade Tiger
#108 The Secret of the Tibetan Treasure
#110 The Nutcracker Ballet Mystery
#112 Crime in the Queen's Court
#116 The Case of the Twin Teddy Bears
#117 Mystery on the Menu
#119 The Mystery of the Missing Mascot
#120 The Case of the Floating Crime
#123 The Clue on the Silver Screen
#125 The Teen Model Mystery
#126 The Riddle in the Rare Book
#127 The Case of the Dangerous Solution
#128 The Treasure in the Royal Tower
#129 The Baby-sitter Burglaries
#130 The Sign of the Falcon
#132 The Fox Hunt Mystery
#133 The Mystery at the Crystal Palace
#134 The Secret of the Forgotten Cave
#135 The Riddle of the Ruby Gazelle
#136 The Wedding Day Mystery

#137 In Search of the Black Rose
#138 The Legend of the Lost Gold
#139 The Secret of Candlelight Inn
#140 The Door-to-Door Deception
#141 The Wild Cat Crime
#142 The Case of Capital Intrigue
#143 Mystery on Maui
#144 The E-mail Mystery
#145 The Missing Horse Mystery
#146 The Ghost of the Lantern Lady
#147 The Case of the Captured Queen
#148 On the Trail of Trouble
#149 The Clue of the Gold Doubloons
#150 Mystery at Moorsea Manor
#151 The Chocolate-Covered Contest
#152 The Key in the Satin Pocket
#153 Whispers in the Fog
#154 The Legend of the Emerald Lady
Nancy Drew Ghost Stories

Available from MINSTREL Books

NANCY DREW® 154

THE LEGEND
OF THE EMERALD LADY

CAROLYN KEENE

A MINSTREL® BOOK

Published by POCKET BOOKS
New York   London   Toronto   Sydney   Singapore

This book is a work of fiction. Names, characters, places and incidents are products of the author's imagination or are used fictitiously. Any resemblance to actual events or locales or persons living or dead is entirely coincidental.

A MINSTREL PAPERBACK *Original*

 A Minstrel Book published by
POCKET BOOKS, a division of Simon & Schuster Inc.
1230 Avenue of the Americas, New York, NY 10020

Copyright © 2000 by Simon & Schuster Inc.

ISBN: 0-671-04262-9

First Minstrel Books printing May 2000

10 9 8 7 6 5 4 3 2 1

NANCY DREW, NANCY DREW MYSTERY STORIES, A MINSTREL BOOK and colophon are registered trademarks of Simon & Schuster Inc.

Cover art by Ernie Norcia

Printed in the U.S.A.

Contents

1   The Parrot's Warning   1
2   Intruder on the Lawn   9
3   A Colorful Clue   17
4   Spying at Sugar Moon   25
5   The Mysterious Meeting   32
6   Action in the Attic   43
7   Letter from the Past   53
8   Diving into Danger   66
9   A Poisonous Plot   74
10 Party Secrets   85
11 Ned's Surprise   96
12 Ants!   105
13 An Elusive Jewel   113
14 Boating Toward Disaster   120
15 A Bid Against Evil   133

THE LEGEND
OF THE EMERALD LADY

1

The Parrot's Warning

"Ugh!" Bess Marvin groaned to her friend Nancy Drew as the tiny plane gave a sickening lurch. "Do you think we're going to die?"

Eighteen-year-old Nancy smiled. "A few bumps won't kill us. I've flown in worse conditions and survived. Right, Ned?" She glanced at her boyfriend, Ned Nickerson, who was sitting beside her, his knuckles white as he clutched his armrests.

"Wrong!" Ned said firmly. "I'm with you, Bess. This is the bumpiest flight *I've* ever been on." The plane veered left, then suddenly dipped downward. Despite the clear sky and calm Caribbean Sea below, the plane bounced unnervingly.

"This is it!" Bess proclaimed, her blue eyes wide.

She threw out her arms in a dramatic gesture. "George, wherever you are," she intoned, "I leave you my chokers, my earrings, and my new black miniskirt."

"Get real, Bess," Nancy teased. "It's just normal clear air turbulence." She brushed a strand of reddish blond hair from her face and peered out the window. "We've just reached the coast of Saint Ann. I bet the island's mountains are making these updrafts. But in case we do crash, Bess, I'm sure George would rather have your tennis racket than your clothes," she added. She was referring to their friend George Fayne, who was also Bess's cousin and a skilled athlete.

"George is lucky she's running in a marathon this week instead of being stuck in this tin bird with us," Bess said gloomily.

The plane headed into a mountain pass. A blast of air slammed up from below, causing the plane to rise, then instantly fall. Bess dropped her face in her hands as the plane skimmed the tops of some trees.

A strip of runway appeared in the pilot's window. Ned grabbed Nancy's hand as the plane shot down toward it at a forty-five–degree angle. "The pilot mentioned that this is one of the trickiest landings in the Caribbean," Ned whispered.

"I can believe it," Nancy murmured, calmly leaning her head against his shoulder. But she did hold her breath as the plane descended, shimmying violently in the crosswinds.

The plane zoomed toward the narrow asphalt strip, like a bird diving for prey. At the last second the pilot brought its nose up, and the plane jolted on to the runway. Nancy and Ned traded excited grins.

The pilot steadied the plane as he slowed it down, then taxied toward the tiny airport building.

"You can look now, Bess," Nancy said, gently shaking her friend.

Bess lifted her head. "Boy, was that close!" she declared. "I'll need every second of this week-long vacation to relax and recover."

"Well, Sugar Moon Plantation is just the place to relax—it has a private beach, and Jack and Emma Isaacs are really low-key. I'm sure you'll feel great the second we get there," Nancy said.

Bess frowned skeptically. "A private beach? I don't know, Nan. How will I ever meet guys?"

Nancy shot Bess a sly look. "There's one next door. Jack Isaacs told me their neighbor's nephew is visiting from Paris. He's a college student taking a year off, and he's been helping Jack fix up Sugar Moon in his spare time."

"From Paris?" Bess echoed, looking pleased. She shook back her long blond hair and added thoughtfully, "Hmm. Did Jack say whether or not he's cute?"

* * *

3

After collecting their bags, the three friends hailed a cab to take them to Sugar Moon Plantation. Jack and Emma Isaacs, clients and friends of Nancy's father, Carson Drew, had bought the run-down sugarcane plantation six months earlier. According to Carson, the Isaacses had been working hard to fix up the place so they could finally invite houseguests. Nancy, Ned, and Bess were their first ones.

When the taxi pulled into the narrow rutted driveway, Nancy was surprised to see how much work the Isaacses still had to do. The front gates were falling off their hinges, and the overhanging tangle of banana and tamarind trees blotted out the sky.

"Do you think this is the right place?" Bess asked as thick vines lashed at the taxi's windows. Huge pricker bushes with inch-long thorns clawed the windshield like the fingers of a skeleton.

"I know the Isaacses bought a fixer-upper, but this driveway seems like a road to nowhere," Ned commented.

"This is a perfect setting for a mystery," Bess murmured, knitting her brow. "Uh-oh—forget I said that, Nan," she added, casting a nervous look at her friend. "I mean, you may be an ace detective and everything, but we've come here to get a break from stress, not get involved in a mystery."

Nancy laughed. "I'll do my best to avoid a mystery this time, Bess. I'm up for a vacation as much as you are."

Just then the driveway opened into a circle, and a huge cream-colored stucco mansion loomed ahead of them. Nancy blinked. The house appeared to be deserted. White shutters dangled from window frames, and balusters were gone from second-floor balconies like missing teeth. Even from the car, Nancy could see huge cobwebs wafting out from the corners of the front portico in the late-afternoon breeze.

"This place looks totally haunted," Bess announced. "The Isaacses *couldn't* live here. Aren't they well-known interior designers who write books on the subject? They wouldn't be caught dead inviting guests to a creepy place like this."

The front door creaked open, and a man and woman in their early forties appeared on the portico.

"Hey, kids," the man said warmly. "Welcome to Sugar Moon."

"Let us help you with your bags," the woman added, heading for the trunk of the cab.

In seconds everyone was standing in the front hall of the house, surrounded by suitcases, while the taxi headed back down the drive.

Jack Isaacs, an easygoing man with sandy-colored hair and blue eyes, disappeared into the kitchen, while Emma, his wife, gave the teens motherly hugs. Dressed in a gauzy white sundress, with dark glasses perched on top of her short red hair, she looked completely prepared for the sun-drenched tropical weather.

"You are our first visitors here," Emma told them, her green eyes twinkling with excitement. "Jack and I have been working on this place for months. It may not look like it, but we've already accomplished a lot." She glanced around at the cavernous front hall with its crumbling plaster walls, chipped marble floor, and broken crystal chandelier. A marble staircase with a wrought-iron banister curved up to the second story.

Nancy's gaze swept the foyer. The house may have seen better days, she realized, but it still retained an old-fashioned elegance that hinted at the luxurious lifestyle of its first owners.

"This house was built in the middle of the nineteenth century," Emma went on. "Jack and I want to restore it properly, but it will take lots of time and love. So far, we've put on a new roof and fixed all the rotting floorboards upstairs—so I promise you won't fall through."

"Oh, we're not worried," Bess said politely. "I think this place is really cool—there's something romantic about it." She glanced around. "They must have had some pretty awesome parties here a hundred years ago—I can just see grand ladies sweeping down that big marble staircase in their ball gowns."

Jack returned carrying a tray of drinks—tall glasses filled with a frothy white liquid. "Here you go, kids," he said. "An island specialty—coconut and pineapple juice mixed in a blender. Why don't we sit on the veranda and chat? I'm sure you'll want to relax after your long trip."

Nancy, Ned, and Bess followed their hosts through a sitting room and out through open French doors onto the veranda. Below them, a wide lawn swept down to Sugar Moon Bay, a gorgeous expanse of shimmering turquoise water at the bottom of a steep hill.

"Have a seat," Emma said, indicating the white wooden deck chairs. They all sat down, and Emma leaned back, stretching her legs. "I love it here," she went on. "Of course, I miss my friends in River Heights, but I've always adored traveling and having adventures. Jack and I bought this place to use as a base for sailing during the winter months. We plan to return to River Heights during the hot season to work on our interior design books. Jack takes the photos while I write," she explained to Ned.

"What a great life," Ned commented, pushing a lock of brown hair off his forehead.

"It's not bad," Emma agreed. "We take our vacation during the winter months and work during the summer—kind of a backward schedule."

"Do you ever plan to put this house in one of your books?" Bess asked. "I mean, someday?"

"Someday, yes," Jack said. "But now it's barely in shape for houseguests, let alone as the subject of a fancy coffee-table book on interior design."

"It's too bad Dad got stuck with a case at the last minute," Nancy remarked. "He would have loved to see Sugar Moon."

"A lawyer's life sure isn't eas—" Emma stopped abruptly. Her eyes had flickered toward the lawn.

Nancy followed her gaze. A chill went through her. At the bottom of the veranda stairs stood a strange man, unlike any living person she'd ever seen. Dressed like a ragged pirate, he wore an eye patch and carried a parrot on his shoulder. His arms were crossed belligerently.

The man locked his gaze with Emma's, his eyes burning like two hot coals.

In one quick move, he reached for his belt and yanked out a cutlass. Its sharp edge gleamed in the sunlight. Stepping forward, he shook it menacingly.

The parrot flapped its wings. To Nancy's astonishment, the bird opened its beak and screeched, "Beware the full moon two days hence!"

The man threw back his head. "Well said, Crackers. Well said!" His wild laughter rang out eerily on the soft afternoon air.

2

Intruder on the Lawn

Before anyone on the veranda could speak, the man scuttled off into the bushes edging the lawn. His colorful patchwork shirt faded into the thick greenery.

"Good heavens!" Emma said, sitting up straight.

Jack pushed back his chair and stood up. Pounding his fists angrily on the veranda railing, he sputtered, "Emma! That man is off his rocker. He's always acted strangely, but he's never threatened us before. You've always excused him, but I think we ought to tell Sam McClain about this incident."

"Oh, darling, please sit down," Emma coaxed, relaxing back into her chair. "There's no need to call in Sam right now." She glanced at her guests and explained, "Sam McClain is the sheriff of Saint Ann,

9

and that man you just saw is known as Old Ironbones. He's a harmless tramp who lives in an old
shack on the far side of Sugar Moon Bay."

"Harmless!" Jack exclaimed, sitting down again.
"What makes you so sure? I know he's eccentric and
likes to pretend he's a pirate, but he shouldn't brandish cutlasses at people."

Privately Nancy agreed with Jack, but she listened
politely as Emma sighed and then said, "You're
right, Jack, he shouldn't. I'm surprised by his behavior—he's never done anything like this in the past.
I'm guessing he just got carried away with his pirate
role, but I'm certain he wouldn't actually *use* the
cutlass."

"How can you be so sure?" Jack muttered.

For a moment everyone was silent. Then Bess
said, "I don't understand why he likes to act like a pirate. I mean, pirates were horrible, dangerous people."

"From what I've been told, he had an accident
years ago," Emma said. "He'd been a fisherman—
fishing, along with tourism, is the main economy of
our island—and one day he was knocked in the
head by the boom on a sailboat. He's been a bit off
ever since. He likes to do a lot of pretending, and
for some reason, pirates appeal to his imagination."

"The Caribbean was a big hangout for pirates in

past centuries," Jack explained to the group. "There are lots of legends about them around here."

"Maybe Old Ironbones got wrapped up in all the swashbuckling stories he'd heard, and he likes to pretend he's in one," Emma guessed.

"Why do people call him Old Ironbones?" Ned asked.

"Because he survived his sailboat accident with no broken bones," Jack replied. "Apparently he took quite a knock on the head—lucky for him his skull didn't fracture."

"But he's no longer able to work," Emma said. "He gets financial assistance from the government. He spends his time wandering around the island, collecting stray animals and teaching his parrot to make these strange pronouncements."

" 'Beware the full moon two days hence,' " Bess quoted, giggling. "What in the world do you think that means?"

Emma chuckled. "Maybe that something bad will happen to us two days from now?" She threw up her hands. "I think it's all nonsense. For all I know, there may not even be a full moon in two days."

Jack cleared his throat. "You're not taking the old guy seriously enough, darling," he warned. "I know you love animals, and you appreciate the fact that he cares for them, too. Maybe because I'm allergic to cats and dogs, I'm less willing to excuse him. But don't forget what he did at our cocktail party the other night."

"What happened?" Nancy asked curiously.

Jack frowned. "Well, we hosted this big outdoor cocktail party to celebrate the work we'd done on the house—our lawn had just been cleaned up and the gardens planted. Old Ironbones showed up at the fringe of the lawn, and I gently asked him to leave."

"Which you didn't *have* to do," Emma protested.

"Emma dear, you know as well as I do that Old Ironbones hadn't been invited. He's a loose cannon—I wasn't sure how he'd behave." Jack looked back at his guests. "But instead of immediately cooperating, the old man just scowled and shook his fist at the sky before tromping back into the bushes."

"Maybe he bears us a grudge for making him leave," Emma suggested in a troubled voice. "We might have embarrassed him in front of our guests, and that's why he threatened us today."

"But I took him aside at the party," Jack countered. "No one else heard us. I was very diplomatic." Jack paused for a moment. A rueful smile broke out across his deeply tanned face. "I'm sorry your introduction to Sugar Moon has been a bit unusual, kids. We'll make sure the rest of your vacation is trouble free."

* * *

An hour later Nancy, Ned, and Bess were renting snorkeling gear at the Scuba Shop, a dive shop in the tiny village of Saint Ann.

"Lavender-colored fins would match my bathing suit perfectly," Bess confided to the diving instructor who was in charge of the store, "but since you don't have them, the pink ones will have to do."

"I've never seen lavender diving gear," the diving instructor said thoughtfully with a trace of a French accent. "But don't worry, you'd look lovely in anything." He smiled flirtatiously at Beth before grabbing two pink fins, a pink snorkel, and a pink mask from behind the counter and handing them to her.

Nancy jabbed Ned in the ribs, then whispered, "Bess already has this guy wrapped around her finger. He's dark-haired, cute, French, I think. What more could she want?"

"Isn't the Isaacses' neighbor's nephew French, too?" Ned murmured.

"The Isaacses?" the diving instructor cut in, leaning toward Ned. "I'm sorry, I don't mean to eavesdrop—but I just overheard you say their name. You see, I'm spending the year with my aunt and uncle, neighbors of Jack and Emma Isaacs. I know the Isaacses well."

"So *you're* the Isaacses' neighbor?" Bess said happily. "Then I've heard all about you." Glancing at him from under her lashes, she added demurely, "Only good things, of course."

"Aha!" the diving instructor exclaimed, his brown eyes flashing. "I realize now who you all are—Jack and Emma's houseguests. They told me you were coming. Allow me to introduce myself. I'm Pierre Lavaud." He shook hands with them as they told him their names. "I'm glad that you came into the shop today. I'm only here at the beginning and end of the day three days a week."

"Because you give diving lessons the rest of the time?" Nancy asked.

Pierre chuckled self-consciously. "I only give diving lessons on the three days I work. The other days . . ." His voice trailed off for a moment. "You see, I attend college in Paris, but I'm not much of a student. An expert diver, *oui*. So I'm taking the year off to teach diving on Saint Ann. I'm supposed to be writing some history papers on the days I don't work, but schoolwork can always wait. There are too many interesting distractions." He winked at Bess.

"Let's finish getting our snorkeling stuff," Ned said a bit impatiently. "It's late, and I want to get out on the reef."

Pierre looked shocked. "But you're not thinking of going out today, my friends?" He glanced at the clock on the wall. "It's almost five o'clock—feeding time for the fish. Who knows what might be out

14

there scouting for a good meal? Sharks are not un-heard of, and barracuda are—how do you say?—'a dime a dozen.' "

Bess paled. "Barracuda?" She pushed her snorkeling equipment back across the counter toward Pierre. "No thanks. You won't catch me being fish food."

"Come on, Bess," Nancy chided. "Snorkeling is a super safe sport. We'll just look at reefs and fish close to shore. I promise we won't ever go out at feeding time."

"Nancy's right, Bess," Pierre said. "You'll be missing a spectacular underwater world out there if you don't go. And the snorkeling equipment is good for the whole week, so you'll have lots of daytime hours ahead of you to snorkel without worrying about predators." Pushing the snorkeling gear back toward Bess, he added, "Tomorrow's my day off. I'll be free to show you my favorite reef. May I meet you at Sugar Moon Bay around eleven o'clock?"

Nancy shrugged. "Why not? I'd like to get a tour of some reefs from an expert."

Gathering up her equipment, Bess tossed it into a large net with Ned's black equipment and Nancy's green. "I'll do it," she declared, "but if there's anything that looks like a barracuda, no matter how tiny, I'm spending my snorkeling time out of the water working on my tan."

* * *

15

"I sure am glad we got our snorkeling stuff today instead of tomorrow," Bess said as she, Ned, and Nancy drove back to Sugar Moon with Jack Isaacs. "Otherwise we wouldn't have met Pierre. I mean, he's so cute . . . and that accent!"

"Oh, you would have met him eventually," Jack remarked as he brought his Jeep to a stop in front of the house. "He's been helping me fix up this place in his spare time."

"So we were meant to meet," Bess gushed as they climbed out of the car.

Ned and Bess helped Jack carry in the groceries he'd bought while Nancy brought in the snorkeling gear. As they stepped inside the front hall, a sudden scream erupted from upstairs. Nancy shuddered as it echoed off the moldy walls of the old house.

"Emma!" Jack cried.

3

A Colorful Clue

Nancy dropped the snorkeling gear and rushed for the stairs. Emma had sounded terrified.

"Wait for me, Nancy!" Jack commanded. "A burglar could be up there—you shouldn't go first." He rushed ahead, taking the steps two at a time, while Nancy, Ned, and Bess bounded up behind him.

In the second-floor hall, Emma was slumped against the doorjamb of the master bedroom. Her arms were circled around her stomach, and her face had a slight greenish cast. She didn't look frightened, Nancy thought, so much as disgusted.

Without a word, Emma pointed inside the bedroom. Nancy followed Jack inside.

They both did a double take. Swarming across

17

Emma's bureau by the door were masses of tiny red ants. The bureau seemed alive as the ants crawled over it. Nancy felt her stomach turn.

"Gross!" Bess exclaimed as she and Ned joined Nancy and Jack. She stared wide-eyed at the ants, which were marching relentlessly in a line from the open balcony window to the bureau.

"You said it, Bess," Jack said, staring at the ants with distaste. "Why don't you guys go find yourselves a snack or something? I can get rid of these critters in no time." He disappeared into the adjoining bathroom.

"A snack?" Bess said, looking green. "I don't think I'll ever eat again."

"Not even the tiniest chocolate-covered ant?" Ned joked, fondly giving Bess a gentle punch on the arm. Bess made a face while Ned added, "Okay, we won't raid the kitchen then, but why don't we put away the snorkeling gear and leave Nancy alone to check out the room? She has on her let-me-investigate look that we all know so well."

Nancy laughed. "I would love a minute to snoop around, guys," she told them in a low voice. "I'm sure it's just a bunch of ants that discovered leftover crumbs or something, but I'm curious to see if there's any evidence that Old Ironbones was here. He could be playing a prank."

While Bess and Ned slipped through the doorway

past Emma, Jack returned from the bathroom with a sponge and a pail full of sudsy water that smelled like disinfectant. He mopped up the floor and the ants. He sprayed, then quickly wiped off the bureau with a chemical to kill ants because water would ruin the wood.

Nancy roamed around the room. It was painted in tropical pastel colors—lemon yellow walls and a sky blue ceiling. An antique four-poster bed with a lacy canopy stood against the far wall, neatly made up with a peach-colored bedspread. A wooden ceiling fan stirred the warm air, ruffling some papers on a desk. Perched in the center of what was probably Jack's bureau was a photograph of a younger Emma in a lace wedding dress. Nancy saw nothing that seemed to be out of place.

A wastepaper basket below Emma's bureau caught her eye. The only object in it was an empty white plastic cup. Stooping down, Nancy lifted the cup to her nose. It smelled strongly of lemonade.

"There, that's done," Jack announced as he gave one more swipe to the floor where the trail of ants had been. "No more bugs, Emma. You can come in."

Emma stepped into the room, obviously relieved. She was followed by Bess and Ned.

"We came back to see if you'd found out anything," Bess whispered to Nancy.

Nancy shook her head, while Emma said, "I'm

sorry to be such a wimp, everyone. I'm not afraid of most things, but ants really get to me."

"Are the ants on this island poisonous?" Bess asked.

"No," Emma answered, "but they're totally determined. Nothing stops them, and they do bite."

"So I noticed," Jack said grimly, pointing to several red bumps on his arm.

"That's terrible, darling," Emma said, examining the bites. She slipped an arm around her husband's waist. "Thanks for cleaning up. Any idea what attracted them to my bureau? I never eat or drink in this room."

"I found a cup in the wastepaper basket," Nancy said, holding it up. "It smelled like lemonade."

"That's funny," Jack said, sniffing the cup. "I could swear the top of the bureau felt sticky when I wiped it off—like spilled lemonade."

"But I haven't been drinking lemonade," Emma protested, "and I've never seen that plastic cup before. Have you, Jack?"

"No," Jack said. He knit his brow and added gravely, "I bet our intruder is at it again, Emma."

Nancy perked up. "Intruder?" she asked.

Emma's face paled under her freckled skin. She sat down on the bed and lay back, rubbing her forehead wearily with one fist. "Do we have to bring this up now, Jack? It's such a bore."

"But I might be able to help," Nancy offered, sitting down beside Emma. "Uh, I've had a little experience with detective work."

"A *little* experience!" Emma said, sitting up and beaming at Nancy. "You're being very modest, Nancy. I know all about your accomplishments from your dad. But I don't want to bother you with our little problem—I'm sure it's nothing."

"Why don't you at least tell me about it," Nancy suggested. "That way, you can get it off your chest."

Emma smiled fleetingly, but her expression was concerned. "Okay," she agreed, while Jack gave her the thumbs-up. "But I don't want to put you to any trouble. After all, you're on vacation."

"Don't worry about Nancy," Ned commented with a grin. "A good mystery would make her vacation even better."

Emma seemed to be doubtful, but she took a deep breath and plunged ahead. "There have been other signs, besides the lemonade, that someone has been lurking around Sugar Moon," she told them. "Over the past few days, Jack and I have come home to find bureaus and closets ransacked. We almost had a fire in the attic. Someone left a smoldering cigarette butt there."

"And some of the books I've stashed away in boxes were pawed through," Jack said gloomily. "It's

21

creepy to think that someone comes into our house uninvited and rummages through all our stuff."

Nancy nodded sympathetically. "It's more than creepy," she said. "It's dangerous. I mean, you almost had a fire. Have you found any clues? Something the person might have accidentally dropped?"

"Just the cigarette," Emma said. She paused, then added, "Jack and I wonder if the person is searching for a special antique or papers because none of our stuff is missing. We have a feeling the person may be someone who's familiar with the history of Sugar Moon."

"Does it have a special history?" Nancy asked curiously, adjusting a strap on her yellow tank top.

"Kind of," Jack replied. "See, until we bought it, Sugar Moon had been owned by the same family, the Jenkinses, since 1850. Charles and Victoria Jenkins, Sugar Moon's first owners, came from England to Saint Ann. The island was a British colony then."

"Charles Jenkins bought up some land and built this prosperous sugarcane plantation—Sugar Moon," Emma went on. "He quickly became a very wealthy man."

Bess gazed out the long balcony window to the sea sparkling on the horizon. "So once upon a time this place was quite a spread," she mused. "Not that it isn't now, of course."

Emma smiled. "We have no interest in turning

Sugar Moon into an actual plantation again. Farming is a full-time job. All I ask for is a house that stands."

Jack chuckled, then continued, "Charles and Victoria's great-grandson, known as Old Mr. Jenkins, died of old age about a year ago. He'd lived in this house all his life, and when his estate sold it to us after his death, his possessions were included in the sale."

"We kept the furniture we needed," Emma added, "and moved the rest to the attic. The house was awfully cluttered, so we didn't need everything. We decided it would be better to get some money for the extra stuff by auctioning it off."

"But someone else seems to be interested in it now," Jack observed. "The question is who? And why?"

"What about Old Ironbones?" Bess suggested. "He seems flaky enough to do anything. Plus, he acts as if he holds a grudge against you guys."

"We were suspicious of him, too," Jack admitted. "Or at least, I was. In fact, I already mentioned him as a possibility to Sam McClain."

"But Old Ironbones has never bothered anyone," Emma remarked, "in all the fifty years he's lived on the island."

"He bothered us today," Nancy reminded her.

Everyone was silent for a moment, then Ned asked, "You say someone has been ransacking bureaus and closets, but was anything out of place in here today? Any open drawers—stuff like that?"

"No," Emma said. She moved over to the desk and studied it, then went to her bureau. "There's nothing missing that I can see. I bet the person spilled his—or her—lemonade, panicked, and beat a hasty retreat."

While they spoke, Nancy took one more stroll around the room. She wanted to make absolutely sure she hadn't missed anything.

After picking up the dust ruffle of the bed, she peeked underneath. Nothing. There was nothing behind the desk or on the balcony, either.

She moved back to Emma's bureau and knelt down beside it. In the shadow of one of the legs, something colorful caught her eye. She picked it up.

It was a green-and-red feather—like that from a parrot.

"Look, guys," she announced, twirling the feather between her fingers. "Maybe Old Ironbones was here after all."

4

Spy at Sugar Moon

Emma frowned. "Let me see that feather," she said.

Nancy handed it to her. Peering at the feather, Emma opened her mouth as if to say something. Then she shut it immediately after casting a fleeting glance at Jack.

She placed the feather on the desk. "I'll ask Old Ironbones about the feather when I see him, but I really don't think he's our intruder," Emma said firmly.

Jack's jaw dropped. "Are you likely to be seeing Old Ironbones in the near future, Emma?"

"Well, I might run into him in town," Emma said vaguely. "Sometimes I spot him wandering around the village square, feeding stray goats."

"What makes you so sure he's not your intruder?" Nancy asked.

Emma shrugged. "I don't know. He strikes me as such a lost soul, and his mind is so scattered. I can't see him organizing a search of anyone's house, and I think our intruder has a purpose. He's going about his search more methodically than Old Ironbones would." She turned away from Nancy, clearly signaling an end to the conversation.

Jack looked at his wife quizzically. Nancy had the feeling he wanted to ask her something else but thought better of it.

Hmm, Nancy thought, Jack seems to be uncomfortable pressing the subject with Emma, and she seems to be hiding something from everyone—including her own husband. But what?

Nancy knit her brow. She felt awkward pressuring Emma—after all, Nancy was her guest. She knew, though, that if she could find out what Emma was thinking, she'd eliminate one of the mysteries here at Sugar Moon. Armed with that information, Nancy could focus on the main mystery—the intruder's identity and what he or she wanted.

Glancing at Emma, Nancy decided to leave the subject of Old Ironbones alone for the moment and try a different approach. "Emma, Jack," she began, "have any other people been in the house lately? I mean, besides us and your cocktail party guests?"

"Let's see," Jack said. "There's Rafaella Rodriguez, our cook who lives in a room off the kitchen, and of course Pierre, who, as I've mentioned, sometimes helps me with house renovations when he's not diving. He appreciates having the extra money."

"I haven't met Rafaella yet," Nancy said.

"She keeps pretty much to herself," Emma said. "She's hoping to earn enough money working here to pay for college in the fall. She's been accepted at a university in Florida and is quite excited about it—she'll be the first person in her family to get a college degree. On her days off she works for a caterer, except Sundays when she rests."

"Sounds like she deserves a day of rest, after all those jobs," Ned remarked. "Have you mentioned the intruder to her?"

"No," Emma said. "I don't want her to get the idea that we might suspect her. She's a sensitive young girl."

"Did any of the guests at the cocktail party come inside the house?" Bess asked.

"Only to use the bathroom," Jack said. "And neither Emma nor I paid much attention to who might have been lingering inside a little too long. Since there were about fifty people at the party, it'd be awfully hard to pin down a suspect."

"True," Nancy agreed. "Any other people you can think of who have been in the house?"

"Hmm," Emma said, chewing her lip, "not recently." Abruptly her clear green eyes flew to Nancy, and she smiled. "How silly of us—Jack and I forgot all about Duncan."

Jack slapped his forehead with the palm of his hand. "Of course, Emma! How could we have forgotten Duncan? He was here for hours examining the stuff in every room of this house."

"Duncan?" Nancy asked. "Who's he?"

"Duncan Adams is a local antique dealer who came in one morning to help us appraise our furniture," Emma explained. "We were trying to decide which pieces to sell and which to keep."

"Duncan is quite a character," Jack said. "He originally came from Saint Ann, born to a family of sharecroppers. But he was a brilliant student. He worked his way through college and became a successful auctioneer at a famous auction house in New York City. He's retired from that now, and he runs an antique shop in town called Hidden Treasure."

"Duncan likes to wear white linen suits with an oleander in the lapel, and he speaks with a fake British accent," Emma told them. "But he's wonderfully talkative and charming. He hosts an auction the first day of each month from the warehouse beside his store. The auction is a huge island event."

"Why? Can people get good deals?" Nancy asked, leaning against the wall next to the bedroom door.

Jack let out a guffaw. "Are you kidding? No one gets a deal from Duncan. He attracts customers by making them feel that if they don't shop at his store, they're not stylish. It's snob appeal, I guess."

"That's right," Emma agreed with a wry smile. "Duncan has a knack for making his auction seem like a private club that only those in the know can attend. Of course, absolutely everyone jams in there because they don't want to miss out, and they want to be considered part of the 'in' crowd. So even those people who might not normally buy expensive antiques will go to his auction and buy things, just to impress others. It's kind of a brilliant business ploy, really."

"To be fair," Jack cut in, "Duncan does his share of good deeds. Because he grew up here, he's devoted to the island, and he donates some of his auction proceeds to promote culture here. He's already started a Saint Ann chamber music group, and he's trying to raise money to start a museum of Saint Ann arts and history."

"He's quite the benefactor," Emma said. "He holds the social life of the island in the palm of his hand."

"I wonder if he could be the intruder," Bess said. "He needs antiques for his store and his auction. Maybe he noticed something on the day he was here, like a porcelain dish or a silver cup. He couldn't have stolen it then because you guys were around, so he came back to look for it on the sly."

Jack ran a hand through his sandy-colored hair. "That's very possible, Bess. Obviously, the intruder isn't looking for a large antique, or else he wouldn't need to rummage through our stuff." Turning to Emma, he asked, "Darling, do you remember if there was a small but valuable item that Duncan saw the day he came—something that you might have put away since?"

Emma's eyes lit up. "That adorable set of silver coffee spoons that Duncan raved about—engraved with Victoria Jenkins's monogram. Duncan appraised them at a hefty price, and later I put them away in a locked pantry drawer with the rest of the silver."

Jack nodded. "That's certainly a possibility. Fortunately, our intruder hasn't bothered snooping around the kitchen area yet."

Listening carefully, Nancy agreed that Duncan could be guilty. But she also realized that if he did steal something from Sugar Moon, he wouldn't be able to sell it at his auction or his store. The Isaacses would recognize it, and he'd never take that risk. Maybe he's looking for something he can sell directly to a private collector. Nancy made a mental note to put Duncan high on her list of suspects.

A rustling sound behind her caught Nancy's attention. Turning, she saw a dark form darting back from the doorway.

Nancy stepped into the hall, just in time to see a tall girl with long black hair disappearing around a corner.

Nancy blinked. Long colorful feather earrings dangled from the girl's ears, feathers that were exactly like the one Nancy had found under Emma's bureau.

5

The Mysterious Meeting

Nancy hurried after the girl. At the end of the hall were two narrow staircases across from each other. The one on the left led up, and the one on the right led down. Nancy turned right, following the girl.

After the bright sunlight that poured into Jack and Emma's room and the upstairs hall, the back stairs seemed dim. Nancy crept carefully down the creaky tunnellike passage. She heard no other footsteps.

Seconds later Nancy turned a corner and emerged into a large kitchen. She blinked at the sudden daylight streaming in through the windows. Then she quickly took stock of the situation.

The kitchen had white wooden cabinets that were chipped and old-fashioned appliances, including a refrigerator with a curved door that looked vintage 1950s. Pink Formica that had seen better days covered the counters. There was no dishwasher in sight.

Nancy drew in a deep breath. The kitchen smelled wonderful, she thought—a mixture of jasmine wafting in through the open window and spicy roasting chicken.

Dishes banged in an adjoining room. The dark-haired girl made a sudden appearance through the doorway holding a pile of plates.

The girl dropped them with a clatter on a nearby counter while Nancy gritted her teeth, expecting the pile to cascade to the floor at any second. The girl, oblivious to both Nancy and the plates, bustled around the kitchen, placing sprigs of mint in iced tea glasses.

"Oh no!" she exclaimed, tossing a mint sprig into the air and rushing to the stove. She lifted the lid on a steaming pot and stirred the contents with a spoon, peering at it intently. "Whew! It's not too burned," she muttered to herself. "At least, no one else will be able to tell."

"Hello," Nancy said quietly.

The girl whirled around, dropping the spoon in the pot. She held the lid in front of her like a shield. "Who are you?" she asked in alarm.

Nancy studied the girl's fawnlike dark eyes, wide

33

expressive mouth, and tea-colored skin. Her parrot feather earrings swung against her long graceful neck. She was very pretty, Nancy thought, with her slim figure and silky black hair. Nancy guessed they were about the same age.

"I'm Nancy Drew," she replied. "I'm a guest." When the girl continued to stare, Nancy went on, "I didn't mean to startle you, but when I saw you in the hallway upstairs, I thought you might need something. I came to see if I could help."

"Help? No," the girl said. "Thanks, but I prefer to do the cooking by myself."

"I didn't mean help you with the cooking," Nancy explained. "I meant if I could answer a question for you or help you find something."

"I don't understand. I wasn't trying to find anything upstairs."

Nancy had a feeling that the girl knew exactly what she meant, but for some reason the girl was avoiding saying why she had been hovering around the second-floor hall. Had she been snooping in other rooms while everyone else had been talking in the master bedroom? Nancy wondered. Had she been eavesdropping on them? "Are you Rafaella?" Nancy asked her.

The girl looked surprised, like a deer caught in headlights. "Yes," she said uncertainly. "My name is Rafaella Rodriguez. How did you know that?"

"The Isaacses mentioned you. They said you're a wonderful cook," Nancy fudged.

"Oh," the girl said, flustered but pleased. She dropped the lid back on the pot with a clang. "That's so kind of them."

"So what were you doing upstairs?" Nancy pressed.

There was a pause, as if Rafaella was trying to invent the right answer. "I came to tell the Isaacses that dinner would be ready in fifteen minutes," she finally said.

"But . . . then why didn't you tell them that?" Nancy asked.

Rafaella dropped her gaze. "I suddenly realized I'd forgotten to turn down the fire under the rice," she answered sheepishly. "So I had to dash downstairs before it burned."

Rafaella glanced up again, and Nancy studied her wide-eyed expression. Is she for real? Nancy wondered. Could she really be so absentminded?

"Well, I hope you rescued it," Nancy commented.

"I think so," Rafaella said quickly. "Uh, would you do me a favor, Nancy? Would you mind giving the Isaacses the message about dinner?—only now say dinner's five minutes away." Without waiting for a reply, Rafaella lifted the lid of the rice pot and shook in a huge cloud of pepper.

This is exactly like that scene in *Alice in Wonder-*

land, Nancy thought—when the duchess's cook pours on the pepper. Does Rafaella really mean to put in so much, she wondered, or is she just distracted by my questions?

With a sudden jerk, Rafaella turned her head away from the pot and sneezed loudly, letting go of the lid in her frenzy. It dropped with a thud on her sandaled foot.

"Oh no!" Rafaella cried, kicking it off. She whirled around toward the stove.

"Are you okay?" Nancy asked, concerned. "Did it burn you?"

"No, no, it's the plantains," Rafaella said, frantically attacking something in a pan with a spatula. "I put up the flame on the stove by mistake—I thought I smelled something burning." She turned several dials on the stove and then opened the oven, reeling backward at the blast of heat.

Nancy shook her head, smiling to herself. Clearly, she was only making matters worse for Rafaella.

"I'll tell everyone about dinner," she promised, turning back toward the stairs.

As she hurried to join the others, she thought about Rafaella. Was she really so clueless in the kitchen? Nancy wondered. Or was she trying to head off questions about why she'd been lurking around upstairs? If Rafaella had been eavesdropping, Nancy realized, she might have overheard their suspicions about Duncan. In that case, she might feel bolder about going through the Isaacses' stuff now, because she'd believe that no one suspected her.

Ten minutes later Nancy, Ned, and Bess were eating dinner with the Isaacses in the dining room. It was just after seven o'clock, and the sun was low in the sky, filtering through the pink bougainvillea bushes that lined the veranda.

Nancy had already tasted her spicy chicken and was now sampling the saffron rice, which wasn't too peppery after all. "I can't believe what a great cook Rafaella is!" she exclaimed. "Now I don't need to feel homesick for Hannah," she added, referring to Hannah Gruen, the Drews' longtime housekeeper.

"If you like the dinner, just wait till you see dessert," Bess chimed in. "When I went into the kitchen to get some juice, there was an awesome-looking pie on the counter. Mango, Rafaella told me, with fresh whipped cream."

Jack and Emma smiled. "We were lucky to find Rafaella," Emma said. "She's young, but she always pulls off these marvelous meals. I believe she learned the art of cooking from her grandmother as a child."

"What's this side dish?" Ned asked, glancing at something that looked like fried bananas.

"Those are fried plantains, a Caribbean specialty

similar to bananas. I could eat them all day," Jack said, digging into his plantains with gusto.

Nancy took a bite of salad made with fresh lettuce and bits of tropical fruit. She couldn't remember the last time she'd eaten such a delicious meal.

Putting down her fork for a moment, she thought about Rafaella. More than ever, Nancy suspected that Rafaella's disorganization in the kitchen had been an act. She couldn't possibly be that way at every meal and manage to produce such delicious food, Nancy decided. Rafaella must have been desperate to keep me from knowing why she was really upstairs.

After dessert Rafaella brought out tall glasses of iced coffee mixed with cream. "If you put sugar in this, it'll taste like a milk shake," she told them, smiling.

"Thank you, Rafaella," Jack said. "As usual, this is the perfect finish to another fantastic meal." He raised his glass in a salute to her. "And now," he said to his guests, "let's drink our coffee out on the veranda. It's a spectacular evening, and I don't want to miss it."

"You guys go out," Nancy offered, setting her coffee glass on the table, "while I help Rafaella clear the dessert plates."

Before Rafaella could protest, Nancy got to work clearing dishes. Standing next to Rafaella at the kitchen sink, Nancy said, "Those are such cool earrings, Rafaella. Where'd you get them?"

Rafaella grinned. "At this little jewelry store in town, right by the harbor. I can't remember the name of it, but they've got real cute things. You should check it out."

"I will," Nancy said. "Did you lose a feather from one of them, by any chance?"

Rafaella frowned, and her fingers fluttered to her earrings. "No," she said. "Why?"

Nancy shrugged. "I just wondered. Are those the only pair you have?"

Rafaella's eyes narrowed. "Why are you asking me these questions?"

"Because I found a feather upstairs that looks like a parrot's. I'm just making sure you aren't missing it."

"Well, I'm not," Rafaella said. "As you can plainly see."

"Did you ever take a plastic cup upstairs that had lemonade in it?" Nancy asked.

"Of course not!" Rafaella said hotly. "Only a slob would do that—everyone knows that food attracts insects on this island. Plus, I never go upstairs in this house except to announce meals. My own room is on the first floor off the kitchen, but I know better than to eat or drink there." She turned toward the sink, her back to Nancy. "Excuse me, I don't mean to be rude, but I need to clean up now—or the ants will take over."

"Okay," Nancy said, giving in. "Thanks for dinner—it was great."

Nancy joined the others on the porch. Leaning back in a deck chair, she closed her eyes and sipped the strong sweet coffee.

"Just like a milk shake, huh?" Bess said with a grin. "Jack and Emma, do you think Rafaella would like to live in River Heights at my house?"

Everyone laughed, but a few minutes later Nancy leaned toward Bess and murmured, "Don't forget, Bess, Rafaella's a suspect." In a low voice, while Jack and Emma were chatting, Nancy told Ned and Bess about her encounter with Rafaella.

"Well, if she is guilty," Bess whispered, "we should at least wait till the end of our vacation to tell the police. We wouldn't want to miss out on her meals."

Ned stood up and stretched. "Anyone up for a walk? After all that eating, I could use the exercise."

"You kids go," Emma said. "You don't want us old folks cramping your style."

"Old folks? No way," Bess said cheerily. "Anyway, I'm staying here with you guys while I digest." She leaned back in her chair like a satisfied cat.

"How about you, Nan?" Ned asked, his brown eyes sparkling. He extended a hand to pull her up from her chair.

Nancy grinned as she took it. "I wouldn't miss a walk with you for anything, Ned. Especially on a night like this."

As the moon rose over the bay, Nancy and Ned decided to stroll along the beach. After climbing down a flight of wooden stairs at the end of the lawn, the two kicked off their sandals and waded ankle-deep into the water. Tiny waves lapped the pale sand. Palm trees swayed in the light breeze, and the dusky sky turned the sea from turquoise to emerald.

Ned put an arm around Nancy's shoulders as they stared across Sugar Moon Bay, absorbing the magical scene. Nancy didn't dare speak, for fear of breaking the spell.

She leaned her head against Ned's shoulder and looked up at him. He bent his head toward her, a lock of brown hair falling over his brow.

The bushes at the edge of the sand rustled. Nancy and Ned jumped at the sudden sound. They quickly drew apart.

From about fifty feet away, a dark figure strode out from the bushes. Two dogs followed him, sniffing the underbrush and washed-up seaweed.

"Look, Ned, I think it's Old Ironbones," Nancy whispered.

"Yup. Let's hide behind the stairs and see what he does." Ned pulled her into the shadow of the wooden steps.

Just then a second person emerged, clambering down another set of stairs and joining Old Ironbones on the beach.

"It's Emma," Ned said as he noticed her short red hair glimmering in the moonlight.

Nancy watched, stunned, as Old Ironbones smiled at Emma, then grabbed her arm, pulling her into the brush. In a second the two disappeared from sight.

6

Action in the Attic

Nancy and Ned stared at each other, astonished. Then Ned grabbed Nancy's hand, and together they sprinted toward the place where the beach ended in a tangle of trees and long grass. A narrow path, curving away from the bay, led into the brush where Emma and Old Ironbones had disappeared. The two were nowhere to be seen.

"I hope she's not in danger," Nancy whispered.

"Let's check out this trail," Ned said, pulling her forward.

"Ned, no! Not yet. We might make too much noise in all that underbrush. Let's listen. Maybe we'll be able to hear them."

Ned let go of Nancy's arm as the two stood still,

listening. After a moment of silence, with nothing to hear but the breeze blowing through the fronds of a nearby palm tree, a murmur of voices—a man's and woman's—arose nearby.

"Emma doesn't sound scared or anything," Nancy commented, listening to the woman's placid tone.

"We might be able to hear them better up this way," Ned suggested. Soundlessly, he crept up the beach, staying parallel to the line of bushes and trees. Nancy followed, her eyes trying to penetrate the thick green brush on her right. But even though the moon was bright, she could see nothing in the jungle of trees.

The voices grew louder. Suddenly the bushes thinned out enough for Nancy and Ned to see Emma and Old Ironbones through a filigree of leaves. They were talking together in a grove of palms about ten feet away. Emma was patting Old Ironbones's parrot, Crackers, as he rested on her hand, but with the exception of "I'm sorry" from Emma and "Thank you, Mrs. Isaacs" from Old Iron-bones, their words were unintelligible.

"I can't hear them," Ned muttered.

"Neither can I," Nancy whispered, frustrated.

After a moment Emma handed Crackers back to Old Ironbones, who immediately placed the parrot on his shoulder. Then Emma took an envelope from the pocket of her dress and handed it to the old man. He gave her a smile and a quick salute, and then the two parted, Old Ironbones drifting farther back into the trees.

Emma hurried out of the bushes toward the flight of stairs she had climbed down, missing Nancy and Ned by just a few feet. In a few seconds, she had disappeared onto the lawn above.

"Whew, that was close!" Ned exclaimed, letting out a low whistle.

"You're not kidding," Nancy said, her pulse racing. "I'm surprised she met him here. She knew we were going for a walk and might see her with him."

"We didn't say we were walking along the beach," Ned reasoned.

"Where else would we walk?" Nancy asked, leaving the question hanging in the air.

"So what did you make of that little get-together?" Ned asked, changing the subject.

Nancy shook her head, still baffled. "It's just so weird—Emma meeting with Old Ironbones in secret."

"Maybe she suspects him of spilling the lemonade in her bedroom so she decided to confront him with the parrot feather," Ned guessed.

"Their meeting didn't seem like a confrontation," Nancy remarked. "They acted as if they were old friends."

"True," Ned said. "But why did Emma have to meet him on the sly, instead of at the house with Jack?"

"Because she doesn't want Jack to know about the meeting." Nancy shot Ned a sly grin and added, "Just don't ask me why."

Putting an arm around Nancy's shoulders, Ned ruffled her hair affectionately. Then the two strolled together back toward the stairs.

"So you've had enough of the beach tonight?" Nancy asked, disappointed that Old Ironbones and Emma had wrecked their earlier romantic mood.

"Nah," Ned said, smiling down at her. "I'm just curious to see whether Jack has any clue that Emma was with Old Ironbones."

Nancy grinned. "Me too—let's go on up." But at the top of the stairs, Nancy cast one more look behind her. By now the sea had turned violet, washed silver in places by the light of the moon. The night made the beach and water so mysterious, Nancy thought. It was as if it harbored tantalizing secrets of its own. At that moment she almost expected to see a pirate's galleon slip across the bay.

"So what do you think was inside that envelope Emma gave him, Nan?" Ned went on, breaking into her thoughts.

Nancy shrugged and turned toward the house.

"Money? Papers? Who knows?" she said. "But there's one thing I'm pretty sure of—Jack doesn't know what's in it, either."

"I feel a little sorry for Jack, actually," Ned declared as they walked up the lawn. "What with his wife holding these secret meetings behind his back."

"Me, too," Nancy said. "But we really don't know enough about what's going on to judge Emma yet."

Ned shot Nancy a lopsided grin. "You mean Emma might have a perfectly good reason for sneaking off to meet someone who thinks he's a pirate and likes to brandish cutlasses at people?" When Nancy gave him a playful shove, he added, "But I'm willing to keep an open mind."

Jack's voice broke into their conversation from the shadows of the veranda. "Hey, you two. How was your walk?"

"Awesome," Ned answered, squeezing Nancy's hand.

"Sometimes I can't believe how lucky we were to have found this house," Jack told them as they strolled up the stairs to join him. "Emma went upstairs to take care of some paperwork while I've been enjoying this stunning view."

Ned and Nancy exchanged looks, while Jack continued, "Bess went upstairs too. She said she needed to get her beauty sleep after your long trip here today."

"Hmm, and before seeing Pierre tomorrow," Nancy said, throwing Ned a knowing grin. "But I think I'll follow Bess's example and turn in myself. It has been a long day." Secretly she hoped she'd run into Emma so she could ask her about Old Iron-bones. Her curiosity about Emma was growing stronger by the hour.

After saying good night to Ned and Jack, Nancy went inside and climbed the elegant marble staircase to the second floor. Just as she headed left toward the bedroom she and Bess shared, the door handle of the master bedroom rattled. Nancy turned toward the sound.

Emma stepped out of the room, wearing a lacy white bathrobe. She had an impish expression on her face, like a schoolgirl who had just pulled off a prank. The moment she noticed Nancy, her face resumed its regular expression.

After asking Nancy if she needed anything else for the night, Emma mentioned that she was on her way downstairs to remind Rafaella that there would be five for breakfast. "Sometimes Raffie is a bit scattered," Emma went on confidentially, tucking her hair behind her ears. "She's likely to forget you guys are here."

Hmm, so Rafaella wasn't putting on an act to keep me from hounding her, Nancy mused. Still, Rafaella had been acting kind of suspicious. She could easily

48

have been sneaking around upstairs or eavesdropping. And since she lived at Sugar Moon, she would know when the Isaacses were out and when the best time to snoop would be. As far as Nancy was concerned, Rafaella was still high on her list of suspects.

"By the way, Emma," Nancy went on casually, "when Ned and I were on the beach, we saw you with Old Ironbones. We walked toward you to say hi, but you were too far away."

Emma's face turned sheet white, but she kept her gaze glued to Nancy's. "Old Ironbones?" she said. "I don't know what you mean, Nancy. I wasn't down at the beach tonight. I was up in my room paying bills."

"But I saw you, Emma," Nancy pressed, "on the left side of the bay."

"You're mistaken, Nancy. You saw someone else." Emma smiled coolly. "You know as well as I do that it's hard to distinguish one person from another at night. Now, if you'll excuse me, I'll be running off to catch Raffie before she goes to bed."

Nancy said good night and headed into her room. She found Bess contemplating six different bikinis spread out on one of the twin beds.

"I've just discovered the purple one's a little tight," Bess said grimly, slumping into a nearby chair. "And none of the others really goes with pink. They've all got red in their prints."

"That's okay," Nancy assured her. "Tropical fish

are all these crazy colors, too—you'll fit right in. But, Bess, listen to this." Nancy filled Bess in on what she and Ned had seen at the beach.

Once Nancy had finished, Bess said, "Emma and Old Ironbones? What's going on between those two? Emma keeps sticking up for him, but I agree with Jack. That old pirate seems crazy—and dangerous, too. It's funny Emma doesn't see that."

"Maybe she does and doesn't care," Nancy said.

"I wonder if Emma knows more about the weird stuff happening here than she lets on," Bess said. "I mean, the way she's acting with Old Ironbones—plus, how she lied to you about being with him."

Nancy thought for a moment. Could Emma's actions with the old man be linked to the ransacked house? Nancy couldn't see the connection, but still, she thought, there was no telling.

"I really wonder what this person is looking for," Bess went on.

"Me, too," Nancy said. "One way or another, I'm determined to find out."

After talking for a while, Nancy and Bess turned off their bedside lamps. Snuggling into her bed, Bess quickly fell asleep.

Nancy stayed awake, thinking about the events at Sugar Moon. Except for the whirring of the ceiling fan and the rustling of the breeze through the banana tree outside, the house was dead silent. Nancy sat up. Was it her imagination, or were there footsteps creaking across the attic floor above her?

She held her breath, straining to hear more. After a few moments of silence, a soft thud did sound from somewhere above.

Nancy threw off the covers. She had to find out what was going on upstairs.

Wearing nothing but pajamas, Nancy crept down the dark hall toward the back stairs that led to the kitchen. She remembered noticing a circular staircase across the hall that twisted upward, to the attic, she had assumed.

Holding her breath, Nancy climbed the old stairs. Her heart pounded with each step that let out a horrible creak. The footsteps in the attic grew louder. Maybe the person is making too much noise to hear me, Nancy hoped.

Reaching the top of the stairs, Nancy arrived at an open door off a small landing. She hid behind the doorjamb and peered inside. No one was there.

A light was coming from somewhere, though, enough for her to see that the room was empty. Suddenly the light began to bob around as footsteps sounded nearby.

There was a room off the empty one, Nancy realized. Squinting into the dimness, she saw that the door between the rooms was half open. Someone with a flashlight must be wandering around in that other room.

Nancy scuttled through the first room. Boxes and pieces of furniture lurked in the shadows, looking like fantastic beasts. Careful to avoid them and the mess of books and papers strewn across the floor, she hurried to the partly open door. Holding her breath, she peeked around it.

Nancy blinked in surprise. The flashlight was propped up in a far corner, creating enormous shadows. Nancy realized the shadows were just of boxes and furniture, but they, too, resembled hulking monsters. Her stomach churned.

Nothing stirred in the room. As far as Nancy could see, it appeared to be completely empty except for the litter on the floor. A cool breeze blew in through an open window. Could the person have heard her and left? she wondered. She stepped inside.

Something grabbed her from behind. Before she had a chance to scream, a hand clamped over her mouth. She tried to cry out, but she could only make a low grunt.

Nancy clawed at the person's hand, but before she could tell whether it belonged to a man or a woman, something hard crashed down on her head.

Nancy crumpled to the floor.

7

Letter from the Past

The room spun around her as Nancy fought to re-
main conscious. She shut her eyes tightly, praying
that the pounding in her head would go away.

Footsteps thudded close to her head. Something
clattered on to the floor. Nancy turned her aching
head in the direction of the noise, but by the time
she could focus, the person had left the room. She
listened for footsteps on the stairs. Nothing.

Nancy struggled to a sitting position. "Ouch," she
murmured, wincing at the flash of pain in her head.
Gently, she touched it. Already there was a big
bump on her crown.

In the faltering light cast by the abandoned flashlight, Nancy noticed an old wooden cricket bat on

her left. She picked it up and studied it. A strand of reddish blond hair was caught in a sliver of wood.

So this is what the person hit me with, she concluded grimly. I hope he, or she, isn't still around.

Nancy stood up, holding on to the wall for support. She threw a cautious look toward the door, which was now wide open. Her attacker might be hiding in the other room, she realized, waiting to knock her out again.

Nancy hefted the cricket bat. At least *I've* got the weapon now, she thought gamely.

Her heart hammered as she tiptoed into the other room. She glanced around, eyeing every shadow in the semidarkness. But unless the person was hiding behind a box or a piece of furniture, the room was empty.

Nancy walked to the stairs—again, no one was there. With her head still throbbing, Nancy made her way to the second floor. Shakily, she stood at the top of the main stairway and peered over the rickety wrought-iron railing to the entry hall below. The front door was wide open, its screen swinging in the night breeze.

She hurried down to the first floor and looked outside. She could hear footsteps scuffing along the driveway, but the sound quickly faded into the night.

Nancy bit her lip in frustration. She'd come so close to seeing the person.

Ugh! she thought, feeling her head once more. Leaving the cricket bat by the door, she went into the kitchen and grabbed some ice. After wrapping it in a dish towel, she pressed it to her head and returned to her bedroom. This time, with no more mysterious sounds creaking through the house, Nancy fell asleep immediately.

"Good morning!" Nancy said as she joined the Isaacses, Ned, and Bess at the picnic table on the veranda where breakfast was being served.

"Hi, Nan, it's late for you," Bess chided, checking her watch. "Nine o'clock." Turning to the Isaacses, she confessed, "I'm usually the late riser."

"Well, I have a good reason for sleeping in," Nancy said, helping herself to some melon and waffles. "I was up investigating the mystery."

"You mean the intruder was here?" Jack asked, setting down his coffee cup with a splash. "Did you find out who it is?"

"Almost," Nancy said, "but then I got hit on the head with a cricket bat, and the person ran off."

"No!" Emma exclaimed. "Nancy, that's awful. Are you all right?"

Nancy pointed to her bump. "I'll live, although I might look like some sort of pointy-headed science-fiction creature for a few days."

"But what happened?" Ned asked, getting up to

check out Nancy's head. "Wow! That's some bruise. I hope you used ice," he added in a concerned tone.

Nancy threw him an appreciative smile. "Don't worry about me, Ned. I'll be fine. But what I really want to do now is explore the attic. The person last night might have left some important evidence behind."

"So tell us what happened," Bess said.

Nancy filled everyone in on her brush with the intruder. When she'd finished, Jack said, "You should never have gone up to the attic alone, Nancy. If you'd woken me, I could have called the police. I blame myself for mentioning our problem to you in the first place."

"But if we'd waited for the police, the person might have run off," Nancy said.

"Still, I don't want any of you to get hurt," Jack said firmly.

Emma finished her last piece of waffle and put down her fork. "So is everyone finished?" she asked, pushing back her chair. "Because I think we ought to do just as Nancy suggests—search the attic for clues. The sooner we find out who this person is and what he wants, the better."

Everyone trooped up to the attic and began to search. In the daylight that came in through the windows, Nancy got a better look at the scene of the previous night's attack. In both attic rooms, books, clothes, and knickknacks were strewn across the floor. Bureau drawers were hanging open, with much of their contents jumbled on the floor. The flashlight, now dead, still sat in the corner of the far room.

"This place is an absolute mess!" Emma cried. "I can't believe that someone would do this to us."

Jack shook his head, puzzled. "I don't even know where to begin. Nancy, you're the boss here. Tell us what to do."

Nancy laughed. "There's no science to it. You just have to enjoy snooping. Let's begin by checking in boxes, bureaus, and closets, and keep an eye out for anything that seems as if it doesn't belong."

"Aye, aye, Detective Drew," Jack said with a mock salute. He began to poke around in a box.

Nancy headed toward a large wardrobe in the corner, while Emma, Ned, and Bess wandered off to hunt through various boxes and bureaus.

Inside the wardrobe were clothes in old plastic garment bags with empty mothball hangers, the mothballs long since evaporated.

Nancy unzipped one of the bags and examined the clothes. They were from the 1920s, she thought—sequined dresses, feather boas, and a little boy's sailor suit. She searched the pockets but found nothing in them.

Closing the wardrobe door, she moved to a nearby box. Heaps of bank statements lay inside—old Mr. Jenkins's bank records from the 1950s, Nancy learned after studying the first one.

A half an hour went by while everyone hunted through the attic for any little clue or bit of information. After finishing with the bank statements, Nancy moved on to a box of books. The books were placed in neat piles, and Nancy guessed that the intruder hadn't gone through them yet. Most of them were poetry anthologies mildewed with age. She started to leaf through one.

Emma sighed and stood up. "I haven't found a single clue," she complained. "I could use a break. Why don't we take the *Starfish* out for a morning sail to get our minds off last night's attack? It's such a gorgeous day."

"Good idea, darling. I'll help you set up the boat. The rest of you can join us in a few minutes. It's a shame to stay cooped up all day," Jack said.

As he spoke, Nancy caught sight of something white poking out from one of the volumes at the bottom of the box. A bookmark? she wondered.

She picked up the book and peered at its worn leather cover. It was an anthology of love poetry. As Nancy flipped it open, a clump of folded papers fell out, the paper old and crinkly with age.

Nancy unfolded the papers and studied the faded

ink on the first page. It was a letter dated April 5, 1870. A whiff of lilac-scented perfume rose from it, mingling with the musty scent of the old book.

"My darling Giles," the letter began. "How are you faring in that dark cruel place? Not an hour goes by when my heart doesn't ache for you. But I know that prison bars can never capture your dauntless spirit."

Giles? Nancy wondered. Could he be Charles Jenkins's son? She scanned the letter for a last name, but there was no surname anywhere. Nancy continued reading, struck by the romantic tone of the letter.

My parents and brother are completely absorbed with the running of our plantation. They live only for money. I don't think they even know the meaning of love! But I don't need them now.

You have taught me what love means, my dearest. Now, whenever the moon rises above the bay, I think of you. I long to be in your arms again. I know your strength would comfort me in my sickness. I want to gaze into your black eyes that laugh at a world that will never understand us. I'll miss you forever.

Consumption is a dreadful disease. I have only a few more days to live. Until yesterday, I'd gaze hourly at the E.E., that special symbol of our eternal love that you slipped into my hand at our final meeting. It's the only thing that has brought me relief from my terror and heart-break. My fate, alas, is all too certain.

Darling, I want you to know where I've hidden it, so that if you ever escape from prison, you alone will be able to find it. If this letter is read by a prison guard, only you will understand my clues.

You'll find it in one of these six places:

1) Under a creaky floorboard near the window where I'd watch for your ship by night. 2) Inside our favorite wishing well. 3) Buried twelve inches under the mango tree where you and I first kissed.

Nancy turned the page—the third one—eager to read to the end. To her surprise, she'd returned to page one. She rubbed each page between her fingers to make sure that none had stuck together but found no extras.

Nancy felt a surge of frustration. The rest of the letter was missing!

"Nancy," Bess said, cutting into her thoughts, "aren't you coming with us? The Isaacses left five minutes ago to get the boat ready."

Nancy glanced up from the letter, blinking while

she focused on Bess, Ned, and the attic room. She'd been so absorbed, she'd practically forgotten where she was.

"Look what I found, guys," she said excitedly, thrusting the letter at Bess and Ned. The two took it and started reading.

"Wow!" Bess exclaimed when she'd finished. "This is the saddest, most romantic thing I've ever read. Don't you think so, Ned?"

"It's a toss-up between that and the instructions to my latest video game," Ned said with a grin.

Bess rolled her eyes and handed the letter back to Nancy.

"Let's hurry down to the bay to show this to the Isaacses," Nancy urged, slipping it into the pocket of her cutoff jeans. "I'm dying to know if they know who Giles is!"

Five minutes later Nancy, Ned, Bess, Emma, and Jack were standing on the dock, which jutted out into Sugar Moon Bay.

"Look what I found upstairs," Nancy said, handing the letter to Emma. "Would you mind reading it and telling us if you know who Giles is and also who may have written it?"

Side by side, Emma and Jack read the letter with growing excitement. Finally Emma looked up, beaming. "What a great find, Nancy," she said. "I'm betting this letter is from Miranda Jenkins, old Mr.

Jenkins's great-aunt. She was the daughter of Charles and Victoria, Sugar Moon's original owners."

"Duncan Adams was telling us all about her the other night," Jack went on. "He knows everything about Saint Ann's history."

Emma nodded. "He knows all the stories, both old and new. Anyway, according to Duncan, Miranda was gorgeous—and quite the free spirit. He said she was a real romantic, and she was known for having these haunting emerald-colored eyes. Men fell in love with her right and left."

"Legend has it that she fell in love with Giles Wentworth, a notorious pirate in the Caribbean," Jack added.

"A pirate?" Bess cut in. "This is wild."

"Please don't tell us he's Old Ironbones's ancestor," Ned said dryly.

Jack laughed. "Duncan would have mentioned that if he was. Anyway, when the police of Saint Ann got wind of their romance, a trap was set. Through a household spy, the sheriff learned that Miranda planned a rendezvous with Giles down at the beach one midnight. Without her knowledge, of course, they used Miranda as bait. When Giles appeared on the scene, the sheriff grabbed Miranda and threatened to shoot her if Giles didn't surrender. Then the sheriff and his men captured Giles, and that was how he was imprisoned."

"But that's so cruel," Bess said indignantly. "And how could Miranda's parents have allowed that?"

"Either they didn't know the plans, or else they were so horrified that Miranda was in love with a pirate that they washed their hands of her," Emma replied. She looked once more at the letter, frowning. "Hmm, I wonder. The E.E.," she said thoughtfully.

"Do you know what it is, Emma?" Nancy asked eagerly.

"I think I might," Emma said. "See, after Giles was captured, the sheriff recovered stolen treasure from his ship. But a famous emerald necklace, known as the Eaton Emerald, was never found. Giles had stolen it from a wealthy American widow, Mrs. Felix Eaton. This letter hints that Giles gave the necklace to Miranda."

"It would figure that Giles gave Miranda an emerald necklace to match her beautiful green eyes," Jack said.

"That is the most romantic story I've ever heard. It's also pretty sad when you realize Giles never received this letter," Bess said, her eyes shining.

"How do you know he never got it?" Ned asked.

"How could it be here if Giles had gotten it?" Bess reasoned. "The whole story reminds me of that poem 'The Highwayman.' Except in the poem, the girl, whose name is also Bess by the way, warns her lover that the police are waiting for him by shooting herself. She was bound and gagged, but she could at least reach the gun."

"At least?" Nancy said, arching a brow. "It would have been better if she hadn't been able to reach it. The highwayman would have been arrested, but she'd still be alive."

"You mean you wouldn't make that sacrifice for me, Nan?" Ned teased.

"No way," Nancy said with a grin. "But since you're not a highwayman, Ned, I'll never be faced with that choice."

"I'm glad that Miranda didn't get herself shot," Emma said, putting the letter in the pocket of her shorts. "That shows she had some sense."

"If she'd been shot, she would never have written this amazing letter," Bess pointed out.

"Speaking of the letter," Nancy said uneasily. "I'm wondering if the person in the attic might have found the page with the last three clues. Miranda might have mentioned Giles's name on that page, and if the thief knows who Giles was, he or she might guess that the clues have something to do with pirate's treasure. Maybe the person will still try to find the first part of the letter."

"That's possible," Jack agreed, nodding. "It figures that someone would turn an attic upside down in an effort to find clues to a treasure."

A chill went through Nancy as she remembered the night before. Her attacker seemed to be determined to find the necklace at all costs.

If her hunch was right about the person having the other clues, the necklace could already have been stolen—this time by a twenty-first century thief!

8

Diving into Danger

The sound of a motorboat puttering toward the dock broke through Nancy's thoughts. Glancing toward the bay, she saw a handsome, dark-haired guy waving from the boat's prow.

"It's Pierre!" Bess said. "I can't believe I almost forgot all about our snorkeling plans."

"Miranda's love life was so interesting, it made you forget about your own," Nancy said, and smiled.

"But not for long," Bess said, gazing at Pierre. "I've totally beamed back to the present."

"*Bonjour,* everyone," Pierre called out. "I've packed us a picnic lunch. I'll take you to my favorite reef near a beautiful offshore island. We'll eat lunch on the beach there." He drew up alongside the

Isaacses' dock and threw Jack a line. "I've already met your houseguests, Jack. They came into the Scuba Shop."

"So I understand," Jack said, smiling in approval as he tied up the boat.

"We'll hurry and get our swimsuits," Ned told Pierre. "And the snorkels."

Back in their room the two girls quickly changed into bathing suits.

As Nancy tied the top of her bikini, she said, "I don't mean to sound like a party pooper, Bess, but I'd much rather check out the clues in Miranda Jenkins's letter than go snorkeling."

"But you will come, won't you, Nan?" Bess asked. "I mean, here we are in the Caribbean, and we've barely been outside."

Nancy shrugged. "We have a whole week ahead of us to snorkel. I'm worried that we're in a race against time to find the necklace before our thief does."

"You'd really choose a dusty old attic over the beach with cute Pierre?" Bess asked.

As Bess mentioned his name, Nancy remembered that Pierre had spent time around the house helping Jack.

So maybe it wouldn't be such a wasted day, she realized. She'd at least have a chance to scope the guy out.

"Actually, I *am* looking forward to getting some snorkeling tips from an expert," Nancy fudged. She didn't want to dwell on Pierre's role as a suspect in front of Bess. She knew her friend meant well, but she doubted Bess would be an impartial judge of Pierre.

"Great!" Bess said happily. "Let's go."

Back on the dock, Ned tossed the bag of snorkeling gear on to the deck of Pierre's boat. Then he, Nancy, and Bess climbed aboard as Pierre shoved off.

"We're off!" Pierre announced as he took the helm. His smile was a flash of white against his deeply tanned face. "How do you like the *Pearl of the Seas* so far? She's beautiful, don't you agree?"

"I agree," Ned said.

Nancy explored the boat, which was a small cabin cruiser. Down the stairs, or companionway, was the cabin, with cushioned benches that she realized could be converted into bunks. There was also a tiny kitchen area, or galley, opposite a built-in desk. She took a quick glance at the neat, uncluttered desk and saw only a bill for boat fuel.

"Your boyfriend's taking over as captain for a minute," a voice said behind her.

Nancy tried her best not to start as she turned toward Pierre. "Your boat is beautiful," she said calmly. "Do you live on it?"

"This boat belongs to my uncle and aunt, and officially I live with them," he said. "But they've both got busy jobs, and they are not at home much. So I spend a lot of my free time on their boat. I even spend the night on it sometimes. Of course, I love the sea. The closer I am to it, the happier."

Nancy smiled. "Paris is a landlocked city. You must get frustrated there without the sea."

"That's exactly why I like to be here, on lovely Saint Ann," Pierre said, pronouncing *that* like *zat*. He gestured toward the companionway. "But let's not spend time down here, Nancy. Don't you want to feel the sea breeze blowing against your face?"

They returned to the deck, and Pierre took over at the helm from Ned. As the boat zipped through the crystal clean water, a tiny dark mass in the distance grew larger. "That's where we're headed," Pierre explained. "To the island called Pirate's Rock. There is a cove with a reef—a perfect place to snorkel."

"How did the island get its name?" Bess asked suspiciously.

"In days long past, pirates used it as a base for their exploits," Pierre said. "But don't worry, my dear Bess," he continued, ruffling her long blond hair, "I will protect you."

Nancy raised a brow. "From what?" she asked suspiciously.

"From whatever evil lurks there now," Pierre answered, shooting Bess a flirtatious smile.

As the boat drew closer to the island, patches of purple appeared in the turquoise water. "What are those dark things?" Bess asked, peering at the water through her sunglasses.

"The coral reef," Pierre said. "Here, let me show you." He dropped anchor about ten yards from shore. After motioning his guests down into the cabin, he opened a panel to reveal a glass bottom. Tiny multicolored fish darted around. Then a luminescent silver and red fish wiggled toward them, feeding on the coral.

"They're beautiful!" Bess exclaimed. "You've just sold me on snorkeling, Pierre. I don't need to work on my tan today."

Pierre chuckled. Just then a large, sinister-looking dark object edged into view on the sandy bottom.

"What's that?" Nancy asked.

"A stingray. Watch out for it while you're swimming," Pierre warned. "Just don't step on the ocean floor without looking. And there's a small octopus around, too, but it's quite shy."

Bess appeared to be anxious but said nothing.

"Come, everyone," Pierre said, closing the bottom. "Let's wade to the beach."

Everyone climbed off the boat, toting picnic supplies, a beach umbrella, snorkeling gear, and towels. Nancy noticed that Bess kept her gaze locked firmly on the water as she stepped cautiously toward shore.

Once on the beach, they set up the yellow- and white-striped beach umbrella. Underneath it, they spread beach towels and then sat down to eat lunch.

"I hope you like ham and cheese on French bread," Pierre said, handing out sandwiches, chips, and fruit. "It's a popular choice in France."

"I'm impressed that you can cook as well as sail," Bess crooned, leaning closer to Pierre.

"Slapping together a few sandwiches—I assure you, it is nothing," Pierre said, obviously pleased.

The foursome ate in silence for a few minutes. Then Nancy turned to Pierre and asked, "I hear you've been helping Jack with house renovations. Did you spend any time in the attic?" She studied his face, curious to see his reaction, but he didn't flinch at her question.

"Hmm," he said thoughtfully. "I remember spending a few hours up there with Jack one day, but that's it. Why do you ask?"

"I'm hot, guys," Bess cut in. "Let's go snorkeling." She dug out her flippers and snorkeling mask from the bag and smiled sweetly at Pierre. "I'm ready for a lesson from a world-class expert."

Nancy threw Bess a thankful smile. She knew Bess was trying to distract Pierre so that Nancy wouldn't have to answer his question.

Pierre glowed at Bess's compliment. "I will be happy to show you all I know, Bess," he said proudly.

After putting on his mask and flippers, he led Bess into the water.

"So what are we waiting for, Nancy?" Ned asked. "Let's go in."

Once in the water with their snorkeling gear on, Nancy and Ned swam out about ten yards. After a few seconds Nancy got used to breathing through the snorkel. The clear warm water felt like silk on her skin as she peered through her mask at the underwater world below. Majestic purple and green fan coral swayed with the gentle current, while tiny blue- and yellow-striped fish nibbled on it.

Shafts of sunlight illuminated the water, making the underwater world explode with color. A bright purple fish swam under her, heading for a knobby chunk of coral just ahead, while a school of shiny silver and black fish with long pointed noses swept into a tunnel in the coral.

Nancy and Ned swam parallel to the reef. Its branches, full of crazy twists and turns, reminded Nancy of a palace from a Dr. Seuss book. She couldn't believe the electric colors of the fish and coral—a world all its own under the sea.

After about fifteen minutes, Nancy lifted her face out of the water. She was curious to see where Bess and Pierre had gone. As she pushed her mask up on her forehead, a loud scream cut through the air. It was Bess!

Nancy grabbed Ned's shoulder as her gaze swept the water for Bess.

"Help!" Bess yelled from about thirty feet away. "I'm surrounded—by three giant barracuda!"

Nancy's mouth went dry. She scanned the water for Pierre. His boat was gone!

9

A Poisonous Plot

"Pierre's not here," Ned cried. "We've got to save Bess, quick!"

Nancy and Ned swam toward Bess, their flippers propelling them through the water in a flash. In seconds Nancy saw three dark shapes hovering around Bess's legs.

Nancy didn't know much about barracuda, except that they did sometimes attack humans. These, about seven feet long, looked vicious and ready to lunge at any second.

One of the barracuda opened its mouth to expose razor-sharp teeth. When it saw Nancy and Ned, it shot backward, observing them through lidless eyes. Nancy shivered—it was like a totally alien creature.

Another barracuda plunged toward Bess. She screamed as it darted at her finger. A gold ring she wore gleamed in the water.

Nancy and Ned lifted their heads and spat out their snorkels. "Get your hand out of the water, Bess—now!" Ned shouted. Bess obeyed him instantly, and the barracuda stopped short. Bess stared at the fish, paralyzed with shock.

"Ned, do you have any coins or keys on you?" Nancy asked tensely.

"Yeah, in my pocket. Why?"

"Drop them in the water," Nancy urged.

Reaching into the pocket of his swim trunks, Ned pulled out several coins and dropped them on the sandy ocean floor. To Nancy's relief, all three barracuda instantly dove for the coins.

"Wow!" Ned exclaimed, staring at the three huge fish. Then he quickly refocused on their predicament. "Let's get Bess back to shore!"

Nancy and Ned each grabbed one of her arms and hauled Bess into shallower water. Clouds of sand roiled through the water as the barracuda continued to dive-bomb the coins. "Are you okay, Bess?" Nancy asked as they waded toward land.

Coughing up sea water, Bess nodded. "I'm okay," she sputtered bravely.

Once safely on the beach, Ned asked, "So, Nancy,

how did you know that barracuda would go for those coins?"

After catching her breath, Nancy said, "When the barracuda went for Bess's ring, I figured it liked it because it was shiny." Taking off her flippers and mask, she went on, "So I got the idea that dropping something shiny might distract them for a minute." She flashed him a smile. "But I thought it was a long shot you'd have coins in your bathing suit pocket, Ned."

Ned chuckled. "Well, you never know where a soda machine will turn up."

"Definitely not on Pirate's Rock," Bess said glumly as she plopped down on her towel. "This place is like no-man's-land. And now Pierre's skipped out on us."

"Where'd he go?" Ned asked.

"To check out a reef on the other side of the island. He said it has awesome fish," Bess answered. "He wanted to make sure the current wasn't too strong there for us. He said we'd be safe here without him, and I was just on my way to join you guys when those barracuda showed up."

Nancy scanned the cove. The sun beat down on the beach and the scrubby island vegetation. Other than a few mangroves off to the right, there were no other trees in sight.

"There's not a whole lot of shade here," Nancy commented. "I hope Pierre won't be too long."

Ned shrugged. "How long could it take to check out a current?"

The three huddled under the beach umbrella to escape the broiling sun. They passed around a bottle of sunblock.

After half an hour went by, Nancy checked her watch. "I'm going to walk around that point there to see if there's more shade on the other side." She pointed to the left, where a spit of land jutted into the sea.

Putting on her baseball cap, Nancy jogged down the beach and followed a path over the sandy point. On the other side were three low trees with triangular-shaped leaves and nutlike fruit. It's not the greatest shade, she thought, but it's better than that skimpy umbrella.

Just as Nancy turned back to tell the others that she'd found shade, Pierre's boat rounded the point. From her view on the crest, Nancy watched Pierre guide his boat into the cove. He was close enough for her to see his face.

Pierre's gaze fixed on Ned and Bess on the beach. Was it her imagination, Nancy wondered, or did Pierre look surprised to see them? What was the guy expecting—that they'd all have been eaten by barracuda?

Nancy jogged back to the group as Pierre joined them.

"We were beginning to think you'd been caught in the current," Bess said. "What took you so long?"

"That's exactly what happened, Bess," Pierre said earnestly. He smoothed back his wet dark hair. "The moment I got in the water, I was pushed out to sea. It's a good thing we didn't go swimming there before I tested it."

"That's awful, Pierre," Bess said, jumping up to face him. "You could have drowned."

"But I kept thinking that I couldn't strand you all here," he said. "I told myself I had no choice but to swim out of the current."

Nancy studied Pierre. His voice was shaky, as if he had really been scared. Maybe he's telling the truth, she thought.

"We had an adventure, too," Nancy said. She described the barracuda.

"I can't believe it!" Pierre exclaimed, his eyes wide. "I've never seen barracuda around this reef—if I had, I would have told Bess to take off her jewelry. Barracuda will usually leave you alone unless it's feeding time or you're wearing shiny jewelry."

"We learned that the hard way," Nancy said.

Pierre looked crestfallen. "I blame myself that you fell into this danger. I take complete responsibility, as a certified diving instructor, for any harm you may have suffered. But now you have learned a small lesson—fish are attracted to shiny things, and barracuda are no exception."

Once more Nancy eyed Pierre. He sounded sincere, she thought. Maybe he really did feel bad about the barracuda.

"What?" Emma said, staring at Nancy, Ned, and Bess in shock. "You went snorkeling at Pirate's Rock?"

Pierre had just dropped them off at Sugar Moon, and the three friends had found the Isaacses working in the garden in front of the house.

Jack's blue eyes narrowed as he expressed his concern. "Barracuda are known to lurk around the cove there," he explained. "Also, the only shade on the island comes from manchineel trees. They have deadly poisonous fruit. If you sit under one during a rain shower, you can get badly burned. The water releases acid from the foliage. Pierre should have known better than to take you there."

Nancy looked at Jack, stunned. She couldn't believe that Pierre had lied to them about the barracuda. He had sounded totally honest.

On the other hand, he had been a diving instructor on the island for months. Surely he would know where barracuda congregate, she thought. Also, he claimed the reef was his favorite, so wouldn't he be familiar with the fish there?

Nancy sighed—she'd have to question him. In the meantime, she hoped to check out the three clues from Miranda Jenkins's letter. Maybe they could all track down the "E.E." by the end of the afternoon.

A small pile of dirt caught her eye a few feet away. A trench about a foot deep had been dug around a large shady fruit tree.

Jack cleared his throat. "Uh, if you're wondering what that is, Nancy," he said sheepishly, "I was looking for Miranda's necklace while you were out with Pierre. This is the only mango tree on the property."

"Unfortunately, it was a dead-end clue," Emma chimed in.

"What was that clue again?" Ned asked.

"I know it by heart," Bess said. " 'Buried twelve inches under the mango tree where you and I first kissed.' But what were the others?"

Emma pulled the letter out of her pocket. "Let's see, Bess. 'Under a creaky floorboard near the window where I'd watch for your ship by night' and 'Inside our favorite wishing well.' "

"Well, let's not tear up the floorboards in any of the rooms overlooking the bay," Jack declared. "Not unless we get desperate."

Emma grimaced. "I agree, darling. After working so hard on this house, it would be a shame to tear up anything we've fixed."

"And since no one knows which window Miranda meant, the whole front of the house could get dug up for nothing," Ned pointed out.

"Do either of you know of a wishing well?" Nancy asked.

Jack rubbed his chin as he thought. "Let's see, we've got more than two hundred acres here—most of it overgrown sugarcane fields too wild to walk through. So I haven't been over the whole property, but I can't think of any wishing well on it. Can you, Emma?"

"No, I can't," Emma said. "But I'm not familiar with the entire property either. Most of it is jungle."

Nancy couldn't imagine a dying woman having the energy to dig a twelve-inch hole or pull up floorboards. The wishing well was the most likely clue they had. If they could only find it, she thought, frustrated.

Even if they could track it down, she realized they still might not find the Eaton Emerald. There was a fifty-fifty chance that the other page of the letter held the one good clue. In that case, how would they ever find the necklace?

"I'll keep the letter with me," Emma said, putting it back in her pocket. "So it doesn't fall into the wrong hands."

"Good idea," Nancy agreed. "And now, I think I'll shower and change before dinner."

"Speaking of dinner," Emma said, "I forgot to tell you that we've all been invited to a dance this evening at Duncan Adams's house. He's throwing a benefit for the Saint Ann museum. All the island bigwigs are sure to be there."

"It'll be fun," Jack added, smiling.

"The party isn't for dinner," Emma went on, "so I think we should eat at the Flying Fish. It's a cute outdoor restaurant down by the harbor in town. You kids will get to see a bit of island nightlife."

"Sounds great to me," Ned said as Nancy and Bess nodded in agreement.

Jack patted his stomach over his blue polo shirt and sighed. "Just don't expect food as good as Rafaella's."

That evening Nancy, Ned, Bess, and Emma stepped out of Jack's Jeep in front of the Flying Fish. "That's such a cute dress, Nan," Bess said, admiring Nancy's short white dress that flattered her slim figure.

"Ditto for you, Bess," Nancy said, grinning at her friend. Bess wore a pink silk tank top with a short black skirt and a coral-colored bead choker. Nancy and Emma carried light evening jackets in case the evening grew chilly.

"Hey, Ned," Bess said, holding out a lipstick. "Would you mind putting this in your pocket? My skirt doesn't have pockets, and I didn't bring my purse."

"No problem, Bess," Ned said, taking the lipstick.

Jack joined them after parking the car, but just as

the five were about to enter the Flying Fish, Nancy noticed a jewelry shop next door. "I'll join you guys in a second," she said, and slipped inside the store.

The owner was a tiny, dark-skinned elderly woman, dwarfed by the large glass display case in front of her. "I'm just about to close up shop, dear," she told Nancy in a whispery voice.

"That's okay," Nancy said, smiling down at her. "I just have a quick question. Do you sell feather earrings?"

"Parrots and peacocks," the old woman said, slapping the right side of the counter. "Take your pick." Inside, a pair of parrot feather earrings just like Rafaella's rested on a velvet cloth.

"Did a pretty girl with long dark hair buy a pair of these recently?" Nancy asked.

"She bought two pair," the woman declared. "Just yesterday morning she bought a second pair— said she'd lost one earring and needed a replacement, but I don't sell one without the other. Now, if you don't mind, miss, it's late." She waved at the door.

Nancy thanked her and left. So Rafaella had lied—she *had* lost her earring, probably right there in Emma's bedroom. As Nancy joined the others at the Flying Fish, she made a mental note to keep a close eye on the Isaacses' cook.

When the waitress came to take Nancy's order,

Emma said, "I recommend the fresh fish catch of the day, Nancy. It comes with either plantains or salad. We've all ordered plantains."

"I'd like the fish with salad," Nancy told the waitress, handing back her menu.

After ordering, Nancy glanced around the restaurant. The mood there was festive. Pots of bougainvillea decorated the dock. People laughed and talked at brightly colored tables under a canopy of vines. Moonlight danced on the harbor, while fishermen readied their boats for the night. Goats bleated from the narrow streets nearby.

The waitress set Nancy's salad down in front of her. While she served the rest of the table their plantains, Nancy examined her lettuce. Nuts were crumbled across the top. Some were walnuts, and some were—what? she wondered.

She picked up her fork. But before she could take a bite, Emma whisked her salad away.

Emma's eyes widened with horror as she stared at it. "That's manchineel fruit mixed in with your walnuts—it's full of deadly acid," she whispered. "Someone just tried to poison you, Nancy."

10

Party Secrets

Nancy and the others gaped at Emma, stunned. Then they all began to speak at once. Nancy raised a hand to silence them. She quickly glanced around the restaurant. Diners were talking, laughing, or calmly eating. No one seemed particularly suspicious. No one was even looking at them.

Then her gaze flicked to the bar. Several people were leaning on it, chatting with the bartender. A stout well-dressed man, dark-skinned with graying hair, fixed his eyes on Nancy. A muscle worked along his jaw as she studied him. Could that man have poisoned my salad? she wondered. He's giving me a kind of weird look.

The bartender handed the man a large Styrofoam

cooler. Abruptly he took it and dashed up the restaurant stairs to the street.

"Excuse me," Nancy said, pushing back her chair. "I'll be right back." Nancy wove her way through the tables and hurried up the stairs after the man. As she ran through the Flying Fish gate, the man threw the cooler into a nearby Jaguar and hopped inside. Nancy had almost reached him when he screeched out of his parking space, tires burning.

"Rats!" Nancy said to herself, punching her palm in frustration. "And I didn't even get the number on his license plate."

Shaking back her shoulder-length hair, she fought to compose herself. That man may or may not be guilty, she thought, but I sure would like to know who he is.

Nancy considered the way the Flying Fish was set up, surrounded as it was on three sides by water. The kitchen was separated from the dining area by a small counter. The person obviously sneaked the poison fruit on to the salad before it was served, she thought. But how?

She hurried back inside. The bartender was filling up some tall glasses with soda when Nancy said, "Excuse me. Could I ask you a few questions?"

"Sure," he said, smiling. "Let me just serve these

drinks." After placing the drinks on a tray and giving it to the waitress, he said, "Okay, miss, shoot."

"That older man with the gray hair who was sitting here—do you know his name?"

"I'm afraid I don't," the bartender said in a lilting West Indian accent. "You see, I'm new to this particular island. I don't know many people here yet."

"What was in the cooler he took away?" Nancy asked.

"Several pounds of fresh mussels," the bartender said. "The Flying Fish operates a retail fish store next door. It was just about to close for the night, so he ordered the mussels from here. Luckily, we still had some on hand."

Nancy thanked the bartender and headed back to her table. Her friends were staring at her in shock, their appetizers still uneaten.

"Are you okay, Nan?" Ned asked, concerned.

"I'm fine," Nancy said. "You guys should go ahead and eat. For some reason, this person seems to be targeting me. I'm going to show my salad to the cook and waitress and see what they have to say." She picked up her salad and went into the kitchen, where the head cook was busy broiling fish. "Excuse me," Nancy began. When the cook didn't respond, she said loudly, "My salad has poisonous fruit on it."

The cook shot up from the stove and glared at Nancy. "Say that again, miss?" he commanded.

"Look," Nancy said, thrusting the salad plate under his nose. "It's that poisonous fruit that grows on manchineel trees mixed in with the walnuts on my salad."

The cook grabbed the plate and studied it.

"Well, I'll be," he muttered.

"Do you know how it got there?" Nancy asked.

"Are you accusing me of trying to poison you?" the cook asked belligerently.

"No, not at all. I'm just trying to track down the person who did put it there. Did you make the salad?"

The cook blew out his breath, slamming the plate down on the counter. "I did, but I didn't put poison on it. I mean, who are you kidding?"

At that moment the waitress appeared at the counter between the kitchen and dining area. Nancy immediately told her about the fruit. Her jaw dropped. "Oh . . . I'm so sorry, miss," she sputtered. "I can't think how that could have happened."

Nancy turned to the cook. "Where did the salad go after it was prepared?" she asked.

The cook pointed to a counter behind him next to a screened door. "It sat on this counter while I got the plantains ready," he explained. "Then I put the entire order on this counter for the waitress to pick

88

up." He patted the counter between himself and the waitress.

Nancy peeked through the door next to the first counter. It led into a narrow alley that led up to the street.

"Could someone have sneaked in through this door and sprinkled the poisoned fruit on the salad while your back was turned?" she asked the cook.

"Well . . . I suppose so," he said reluctantly. "Of course, I concentrate on my stove most of the time. I *am* a perfectionist, you see."

Nancy turned to the waitress and asked, "Is there any way someone could have found out that I ordered that salad?"

"Uh, no one questioned me," she replied. "But I wonder . . ." She paused, acting embarrassed.

"What?" Nancy pressed.

The waitress thumbed through a stack of orders impaled on a sharp pick that lay on the counter near the screened door. "Here's yours," she said, pulling it off and showing it to Nancy. "Since you were the only one at your table who wanted salad, I made a note next to your order to help me remember who got what."

Nancy looked at the order slip. Sure enough, next to *salad* was printed, "Blond in white dress." So someone must have sneaked up to the door, seen the order slip, and then sprinkled the fruit on the salad when it came, Nancy reasoned. Someone who just happened to be carrying around a stash of that poison fruit, waiting for the perfect moment to strike.

Nancy thanked the cook and waitress and returned to her table. After telling everyone what she had learned, Nancy finished her dinner halfheartedly.

Emma sighed and put down her fork. "I think we've all lost our appetites here. Why don't we forget dessert and hurry over to Duncan's party? It might help lift our spirits."

"Good idea," Jack said, pushing back his chair. "I'll get the bill, and then we'll go."

Fifteen minutes later Jack pulled his Jeep up to a huge mansion on a hill overlooking the sea. "Wow!" Bess exclaimed. "This place is awesome."

"You're not kidding," Ned agreed. "Mr. Adams's store must be a major success."

"He made most of his money in New York," Emma remarked. "But he certainly doesn't object to making a bit more here."

After Jack parked the Jeep, the Isaacses led the way to the front lawn, where the party was in full swing. The lush grounds, ornamented with pools and fountains, were glittering with hundreds of Japanese lanterns. Gardens with every variety of tropical plant lined the velvety grass. About two hundred people mingled on the lawn, some dancing to a swing orchestra.

"Hello, Isaacses!" a man shouted. Turning, Nancy saw a tall, thin, West Indian man with short dreadlocks approaching them. He wore a white suit and had a pith helmet in his hand.

"Sam!" Jack cried. "I was hoping we'd see you here. Let me introduce our houseguests, Nancy Drew, Bess Marvin, and Ned Nickerson. This is our good friend Sam McClain, the sheriff of Saint Ann."

Everyone shook hands. After a moment of small talk, the sheriff moved off to another group.

"He seems a lot nicer than that old-time sheriff who arrested Giles," Bess commented.

"That's for sure," Nancy agreed.

"May I take your jackets, ladies?" a voice at her elbow said. "When you need them, just let me know."

Turning, Nancy saw a man in a white coat and black bow tie smiling at her politely. She and Bess and Emma thanked him and handed him their jackets. At that moment a gray-haired West Indian man in a white suit rushed over to greet them.

Nancy did a double take. It was the man who had bought mussels at the Flying Fish!

"Duncan!" Jack exclaimed, slapping the man on his back in greeting. "As usual, your party is *the* main event. How go things?"

"Fine, fine," Duncan said, beaming with satisfaction as his eyes darted around the crowd of party-goers on the lawn.

"Let me introduce our houseguests," Emma said. Duncan's gaze flickered over the three teens as Emma introduced them. Nancy shook Duncan's hand warily, trying to get a bead on him.

"So nice to meet you, Miss Drew," he boomed, pumping her hand. But the next moment, his attention drifted to a new arrival.

He's not acting like someone who just tried to poison me, Nancy thought, puzzled. In fact, he hardly seems to notice me at all. Still, this could be an act, she realized, just so I won't suspect him.

After making sure they had everything they wanted, Duncan rushed off to greet another group. Pierre moved in to take his place as the Isaacses slipped off to greet other friends.

"I was hoping I'd see you all here," Pierre said, smiling. He turned to Bess and asked, "Would you care to dance? I want to make sure you don't hate me after I stranded you with the barracuda."

"It'll take more than one dance for me to forgive you," Bess said with a pout. "I'll think about it after maybe . . . six?"

Pierre chuckled and offered her his arm. "It's a deal," he murmured as they strolled away.

Nancy tugged on Ned's jacket. "I want to ask Mr.

Adams some questions," she murmured. "He was at the Flying Fish when my salad was served."

"I'll find us something sweet to snack on," Ned offered. "I'm still hungry and missed having dessert."

Nancy moved off to find Duncan, who was standing next to a giant ice sculpture of a pirate holding a treasure box. He flung his arm across the pirate's chest in a dramatic gesture as he spoke to some friends. "This is a fantastic work of art," he boomed in his exaggerated English accent. "What a waste—it should have been sculpted in stone so we could enjoy it forever." He shook his head sadly.

"Well, your whole party is a work of art, Mr. Adams," Nancy said, cutting into the conversation. "I love the Japanese lanterns you've strung up all around your lawn."

Duncan started. "Uh, have we met?" he asked, peering at her. "You are Miss . . . ?"

"I'm Nancy Drew," she reminded him as the other guests drifted away. "I'm here with Jack and Emma Isaacs."

"Ah, yes!" he said. "How rude of me to forget you. It's just that there are so many people here."

Nancy cocked her head. "But don't you remember me from the Flying Fish? You were staring right at me."

"I was?" Duncan said, surprised. "Well, once

again I was unforgivably rude. I didn't mean to stare at you. To be perfectly honest, I don't remember you there at all."

"I remember you," Nancy said. "I was surprised to see you there because your party was about to start," she added, telling a little white lie.

"My caterers were low on mussels," Duncan explained, "so I offered to run into town at the last minute. The cooks were busy, you see, and I did *not* want to run out of my favorite shellfish."

A throng of chattering guests descended on Duncan. Nancy backed off. Now was the perfect moment to explore his house, she decided. If she could find a clue linking him to the Eaton Emerald or the poisonous fruit, then her suspicions would be confirmed—that he'd known all along exactly who she was.

Nancy wove her way through the crowd toward the house. Once inside, she caught her breath as she glanced around. The empty rooms were chock-full of antiques that looked as if no one ever touched them. I doubt I'll have much luck finding clues here, Nancy thought, scanning the downstairs. It's as if no one even lives here.

She rushed upstairs. In the first bedroom off the hall, several white suits on hangers had been flung over the back of a sofa. I'll bet this is Duncan's room, Nancy thought.

She stepped inside and headed for the bureau where sprays of oleander rested in a glass vase.

Voices echoed on the stairs. Nancy froze.

"What I wouldn't give for that jewel!" a man's voice bellowed outside the door.

It was Duncan. He was about to come in!

11

Ned's Surprise

Nancy searched wildly with her eyes, desperate for a place to hide. Just as she spotted a corner closet, Duncan entered the room. Nancy stepped back, but not before Duncan caught sight of her.

Nancy's gaze faltered under his furious glare. She glanced over at the bureau beside her. To her relief, she saw that its drawers were still closed. Things *could* have been worse, she decided, lifting her chin and looking Duncan squarely in the eye. Five more seconds and he would have caught me going through his bureau drawers.

"What is the meaning of this, Miss . . . er?" he asked.

"Drew," Nancy said patiently. "Nancy Drew. Remember, we spoke outside?"

"Ah, yes!" Duncan scowled at her from under his bushy gray brows. "Just what are you doing in my bedroom, Miss Drew? Please answer me truthfully for I don't like snoops."

Nancy thought fast. "I . . . uh, I got cold and wanted my jacket. Your butler put it away somewhere."

"It got cold?" Duncan snorted. "On a tropical evening like this?" He threw her a scathing look. "You should have asked my butler to fetch your jacket for you. How could you guess where he'd put it in this great big house? Quite frankly, Miss Drew, I'm shocked that a guest of the Isaacses would have the nerve to enter someone's bedroom uninvited." His stout frame quivered with his anger.

"I'm sorry, Mr. Adams," Nancy said contritely. "I just assumed—"

"You assumed?" Duncan echoed with a sneer. "There's nothing I hate more than people who assume too much. You should have asked first." Stalking toward Nancy, he added in a menacing tone, "I forbid you to leave this room until I've checked my drawers. If anything's out of place, I'm calling in the sheriff to deal with you."

Duncan opened each of his bureau drawers and carefully studied the contents. Nancy wanted to scream with impatience as he spent minutes fussing over each article, making sure that none of his possessions had been disturbed. "Isn't that a shame," he said, clucking his tongue as he held up a chipped crystal vial from his top drawer.

Nancy felt a spurt of indignation. Was he going to accuse her of breaking something she hadn't even seen? "I didn't touch that, Mr. Adams," she declared, trying to keep her voice steady.

"I know," he snapped, slamming the drawer shut. "One of my assistants at the store broke it. Naturally, I fired him on the spot. And as for you, Miss Drew," he said, looking Nancy up and down, "I'm satisfied now that you are innocent. Since nothing is missing from my drawers, I see that you have only committed the lesser crime of bad manners, not theft."

Nancy opened her mouth to apologize when Duncan held a hand up for silence.

"Let me finish, please," he said haughtily. "Yes, you were rude to enter my room without asking, but I was even ruder to treat a guest so inhospitably. I assumed you were guilty before you had a chance to prove you were innocent. I committed the hateful crime of assuming too much."

Nancy stared at Duncan. She couldn't believe he was making this ridiculous speech—and also that he was blaming himself.

"Can you forgive me, Miss Drew?" he went on. "To make up for my rudeness, I'd like to ask you to dance. Will you do me the honor?" He plucked an oleander sprig from the nearby vase and stuck it through his lapel. Then, with a smug smile plastered on his face, he crooked his arm for Nancy to take.

Nancy hesitated. Do I really want to dance with this stuck-up jerk? she thought.

"Do say yes," Duncan pressed. "You'll get lots of attention if you dance with me, Miss Drew. I can introduce you to a party full of fascinating people, people you wouldn't meet otherwise. I don't know if you're aware of this, but I have powerful social connections on the island, my dear."

Nancy realized that she'd be able to question Duncan more thoroughly if she danced with him. Sighing, she looped her arm through his, then walked with him out of the room and downstairs to the dance floor.

"By the way, Mr. Adams," Nancy said, once they were dancing. "Who were you talking to outside your bedroom before you came in? I thought I heard another voice."

"Ah, yes," Duncan said. "That was the new assistant at my shop, Hidden Treasure. I was showing him some antique maps that hang on the wall by the staircase."

"But you mentioned a jewel," Nancy said.

"Well, I wasn't talking about a real jewel," Duncan said. "I was referring to a valuable antique pirate map that's owned by a rival dealer. To me that map is an absolute jewel."

Ned marched up and tapped Duncan on the shoulder. "Would you mind if I cut in, Mr. Adams?" he asked politely.

"Not at all," Duncan said, relieved to be able to mingle with his guests again. Breathing heavily from the exercise, he lumbered off to talk to a group of admirers on the sidelines.

"So where have you been all this time, Nan?" Ned asked as they began a slow dance.

Nestling happily against Ned's strong shoulder, Nancy told him about Duncan catching her in his room. "I'm just sorry I didn't get a chance to search more," she murmured. "Mr. Adams seems like a pretty slick guy, Ned. There's something about him I don't trust."

"Yeah, but just because he's slick doesn't mean he took Miranda's letter," Ned said.

Nancy bit her lip, thinking. She glanced up at Ned. "Well, he *was* inside Sugar Moon appraising Jack and Emma's stuff. He could have found the third page of Miranda's letter. Since he knows all about Saint Ann's history, he'd know what she meant if she mentioned the E.E. in it."

"But Pierre and Rafaella have been at Sugar Moon, too," Ned remarked. "They also had the opportunity to find the missing page."

Nancy nodded. "And we can't forget who else has been lurking around there—Old Ironbones."

The music pepped up, and Ned swung Nancy under his arm. Peering up at the sky, Nancy noticed a three-quarter moon. "Crackers was wrong, though," she added as she and Ned drew back together. "It's not going to be a full moon tomorrow."

Ned chuckled. " 'Beware the full moon two days hence'?" he recited. "I wasn't exactly shaking in my shoes about that. I mean, parrots repeat what they're used to hearing, and Old Ironbones probably goes around saying a bunch of crazy things."

"That's true," Nancy said, "but Old Ironbones still could be guilty."

"He could," Ned agreed. "So all our suspects had the opportunity to steal the letter, but what about their motives?"

"Well, Duncan's motive is obvious," Nancy declared. "He's an antique dealer who'd love to get his hands on a famous old necklace."

"Yeah, but owning a valuable necklace could be a big motive for anyone," Ned pointed out. "Miranda *must* have hinted about the necklace on the last page of her letter, or the person wouldn't know about it and be so hot to find it."

"Good thinking, Ned," Nancy said. She paused for a moment, considering the case. "So what else? We know that Rafaella may have been eavesdropping upstairs while we were hanging out in Jack and Emma's bedroom. Oh, and I forgot to tell you—she had lost one of her earrings and replaced it yesterday morning with an identical one." Nancy quickly filled Ned in on what she had learned at the jewelry shop.

"Whoa!" Ned said, his brown eyes flashing. "I bet that was her feather in the bedroom, not Crackers's."

"But it didn't have an earring hoop on it," Nancy reminded him. "Still, the feather could have caught on something while she was stooping over and then broke off the hoop. She did lie to me about losing it."

Nancy and Ned were silent for a moment while they swung around in time to the music. The tune changed from a swing number to a reggae piece. "It must be getting late—the crowd's loosening up," Ned said with a grin. They began to dance fast. Nancy's sandals clicked across the wooden floor.

After a few more songs, they decided to take a break. As they moved off the dance floor to find sodas, Nancy said, "And don't forget about Pierre, Ned. Do you really think he could have been so clueless about those barracuda?"

Ned shrugged. "Who knows? One thing's for sure, the person must be worried that you saw him in the attic, or you wouldn't have gotten that poisonous fruit on your salad."

"And Duncan was at the Flying Fish when my salad was served," Nancy pointed out.

Ned handed Nancy a ginger ale that he lifted from a passing tray. "One more thing, Nan," Ned said. "What do you think Emma is hiding about Old Ironbones? I mean, a parrot feather was found in her room, and she doesn't know about Rafaella's missing earring. So why is she so sure that Old Iron-bones is innocent?"

Bess appeared at Ned's elbow. "Do you still have my lipstick in your pocket, Ned?" she asked. "Remember you were holding it for me?"

"Sure thing, Bess," Ned said, reaching into his coat pocket. But as he fished inside for the lipstick, his dark brows drew together in a frown. "Hmm. What's this?" Along with the lipstick which he handed to Bess, he pulled out a piece of folded paper.

The paper, crinkly with age, rustled as a dry leaf would as he unfolded it.

"What is it, Ned?" Nancy and Bess asked in unison as they peered curiously over his shoulder.

Nancy gaped as she saw the words. On the

paper—in faded ink—was written: "Yours now and forever, Miranda."

The three friends exchanged stunned glances. "It's the last page of Miranda's letter," Nancy said. "But it doesn't have the other three clues."

Bess shot a sideways look at Ned. "How in the world did it get in your pocket, Ned?"

12

Ants!

Ned was completely perplexed. "I have no idea how it got there. Except . . ." He hesitated, rubbing his chin in thought. "Well, I did take my jacket off while I went to get some dessert for you and me, Nan. I was juggling a couple of plates, and I didn't want to spill anything. So I slung my jacket over the back of a chair by that table over there."

Ned pointed to a table in the corner, where an untouched dessert still rested. He threw Nancy a guilty look. "Sorry—I forgot to tell you about it. When you came back from the house I just wanted to dance."

"That's okay, Ned. Someone must have slipped the page in your pocket then."

"I know nothing was in my pocket when I put in

the lipstick," Ned said, "and I wore my jacket the whole time we were at the Flying Fish."

"So the person who sneaked it in must be at this party—either Pierre or Duncan," Nancy reasoned. "I was in the house for a few minutes before Duncan came in, so he could have slipped the page into your pocket then."

A woman with long dark hair swept by them, holding a silver tray covered with hors d'oeuvres. She appeared to be frazzled but cheerful as she served the guests. Just as she was serving a cranky-looking older woman with stiff gray hair, she dipped her tray forward and tossed a deviled egg onto the woman's blouse. The older woman drew her mouth into a tight line as the waitress apologized profusely.

Nancy, Bess, and Ned were astonished. "Rafaella!" Bess said, shaking her head in surprise. "The whole cast of suspects is here except Old Ironbones."

Wearing a white blouse, black bow tie, and short black skirt, Rafaella disappeared into a crowd of hungry guests.

"Hello, kids," a familiar voice called out. "Are you having fun?" Jack Isaacs strolled up to them, holding hands with Emma. "Hey, you look as if a bomb just exploded. Is anything the matter?"

"Ned just got an anonymous love letter," Bess said

mischievously. "A secret admirer put it in his pocket."

Nancy and Ned chuckled while Bess told the Isaacses what had happened. As soon as she'd finished, Emma shot Ned a suspicious look. "So does this mean we've found our culprit and his name is Ned Nickerson?" she asked. "Where have you stashed the rest of the letter with the last three clues?"

Nancy studied Emma. Her skeptical half smile made Nancy think that she wasn't completely joking.

A jolt went through Ned. "Culprit? Me? No way," he said, aghast. "I mean, the stuff at Sugar Moon started before I even landed on this island. Some weirdo put this in my pocket tonight, Emma, I promise."

"I know," Emma said, backing off. "I was just teasing." She flashed Ned an apologetic smile. "But why did the person slip it into your pocket? To frame you?"

Ned shrugged. "I guess. Why else?"

Jack sighed anxiously, then quickly glanced around. When he seemed satisfied that no one was listening, he said, "Uh, I hate to say this, but about an hour ago I noticed Duncan Adams hovering around the table where Ned had put his jacket. He was by himself, which is unusual. That's why I noticed him."

An hour ago? Nancy thought. That would have been shortly before he caught her in his bedroom. So Duncan could definitely have slipped the letter into Ned's pocket then.

Nancy took the ancient, yellowing paper from Ned and studied it. There were some markings in the lower right corner, but in the dim light she couldn't tell what they were.

"I want to look at this letter in better light," she said. She gestured for Ned to follow her to a Japanese lantern dangling from a post several feet away. In a pool of yellow lamplight, Nancy peered closely at the page. She caught her breath.

A skull and crossbones had been drawn in pencil in the corner. In the center of the skull, the words *Nancy Drew* appeared in block letters.

Nancy's eyes flew to Ned's. "It's a warning to me."

Ned grabbed the paper and studied it. Then he gazed back at her. "If you were in doubt at the Flying Fish, Nan, there's no question now—this person thinks you saw him or her in the attic last night. Why else would you be getting this warning?"

Nancy's stomach churned as she searched Ned's face for an answer. But there aren't any answers—yet, she realized. Ned's as much in the dark as I am. It's up to me to figure out what's going on, before the person gets to me—or to the Eaton Emerald!

Bess sidled up to Nancy and Ned. Nancy showed her the skull and crossbones on the letter but warned her not to tell the Isaacses about it.

"I don't want them to worry about me and stop my investigation," she explained.

"Promise me you'll be careful, Nan," Bess said anxiously.

"I promise," Nancy assured her.

"It's getting late," Bess said, "and the Isaacses told me they want to leave. They've already thanked Mr. Adams for all of us, and Emma's gone to get our jackets."

Nancy sighed. She'd hoped to question Rafaella about the earring, but that would have to wait until tomorrow.

As the teens strolled with Jack and Emma toward the Jeep, Bess said, "Obviously, there's one more page to Miranda's letter with the other three clues."

"Yup," Jack said. "But you can bet that our thief won't be putting *that* page into anyone's pocket soon."

The next morning at daybreak, sunlight filtered in through the window next to Nancy's bed. Nancy opened her eyes, unable to sleep more after the strange events of the day before. Sitting up, she glanced at Bess, who was still out cold.

Nancy listened to the early morning sounds of the house. Nothing stirred inside, but colorful, exotic-looking songbirds rustled the banana tree by her window.

Absently watching the birds, Nancy puzzled over the case. She felt extremely frustrated. So far, she hadn't had much luck narrowing her list of suspects. Except for Old Ironbones, all the other suspects had been at the party the night before. Any one of them could have slipped the page into Ned's pocket, though at this point Duncan seemed the likeliest person, she thought.

Nancy sighed—maybe it was time for a different approach. Instead of trying to track down the intruder, maybe she should concentrate on figuring out the first three clues in Miranda's letter and finding the Eaton Emerald.

She had decided that the wishing well clue was their best bet. There has to be a wishing well somewhere on the property that Jack and Emma don't know about, she thought.

Throwing off her covers, Nancy crept silently out of bed and put on cutoffs, a light blue cotton tank top, and sneakers. The house was silent as she hurried downstairs and out the veranda door.

On the left side of the lawn, Nancy searched the overgrown tangle of pricker bushes and trees for a break. Old Ironbones came through here on our first afternoon at Sugar Moon, she remembered. There's got to be a path around somewhere.

After a few minutes of combing the brush, Nancy spotted a narrow trail, its entrance nearly hidden by a thick green vine. Ducking under the vine, Nancy headed down the path. Long sharp thorns snatched at her clothes. Scanning for signs of a well, or even another path, Nancy moved deeper and deeper into the jungle. Will I be able to find my way back? she wondered uneasily, as vines and branches closed in behind her the moment she passed through them.

Suddenly Nancy saw brown through the trees. A wishing well? she hoped. She jogged closer.

Moments later a dilapidated building rose up in front of her. The top of a gigantic wheel jutted out from the far side of the building, where she heard the whooshing sound of a rushing creek. This must be the ruins of an old sugarcane mill, she reasoned. The windows of the building were tall and started about a foot above ground level.

A jolt went through Nancy. Was that a shadow in one of the windows? she wondered. She inched closer. Sure enough, the back of a woman's head was silhouetted in the lower part of the window. The woman had long dark hair.

Nancy held her breath as she sneaked closer to the mill. The woman was sitting down, her back to the open window, her arms behind her.

Without making a sound, Nancy peered through the window behind the woman. She gasped, then recoiled in horror.

Shaking from head to foot, Nancy raced around to the front door of the mill. Flinging it open, she stepped inside.

Bound with heavy rope to an iron beam, Rafaella raised her head and looked at Nancy. A gag across her mouth stifled her scream.

Nancy's skin prickled as she stared at Rafaella's lap. Sprinkled all over her was sugar, while thousands of ants marched toward her!

13

An Elusive Jewel

Rafaella stared at Nancy, her eyes expressing her terror. After rushing over to her, Nancy quickly untied her. The instant she was free, Rafaella jumped up, frantically brushing away ants and sugar.

"Rafaella," Nancy said, trying to calm her. "Here, let me get this thing out of your mouth." Then Nancy marched Rafaella away from the swarming ants.

Once the white rag was out, Rafaella screamed in horror, furiously shaking her arms and legs as if to make sure that every last ant was gone.

"You're okay now," Nancy said gently, putting an arm around the panicked girl. But Nancy herself shivered as she watched the marauding ants mercilessly attacking the sugar. "Let's get out of here," she went on, leading Rafaella through the doorway to the stoop outside.

Nancy and Rafaella sat down on the stone stoop—but not before Rafaella inspected every inch of it for ants. "All clear," she whispered, slumping down in exhaustion.

Nancy sat down beside her. "Everything's okay now, Rafaella. Can you tell me what happened?"

Rafaella dropped her face into her hands and shuddered. "I can't think about it," she said hoarsely.

"It's really important for you to tell me," Nancy said. "We need to catch the person who did this to you. We don't want anything like this to happen again."

Rafaella shivered. Then she peeped at Nancy between trembling fingers. Taking a deep breath, she sat up and said, "Okay, I'll try my best to tell you, Nancy. I woke up this morning to go to the farmers' market." She stopped, her lips quivering.

Nancy was worried that Rafaella might break down again. "Is the farmers' market in town?" she prompted.

"Yes. Farmers from Puerto Rico come to town early, and I like to arrive there first thing to get the pick of the produce." To Nancy's relief, Rafaella's voice grew stronger as she spoke. "Anyway," she explained, "there's a trail through the jungle that cuts over the hill to the paved road where I keep my bike. I have my own pickup truck, but I like getting exercise. But I'd rather not ride my bike down the long bumpy driveway, so I always take the shortcut. I can tie my bike to a tree over there so it stays safe."

She paused, looking at Nancy for encouragement. When Nancy smiled, Rafaella went on, "A few minutes after I started down the trail, I heard noise in the direction of the old mill, like wood breaking. I thought that was strange, so I sneaked down a side trail to the mill to check it out." She grimaced. "I guess I was stupid to investigate by myself, but I had pretty much convinced myself that Mr. Isaacs was getting an early start on some repairs and I was being paranoid to think anything else. But as it turned out, my first guess was right."

She stopped as two tears squeezed out of the corners of her eyes.

"Go on," Nancy said, patting her shoulder. "You're doing a great job with your story."

"Sorry, Nancy," Rafaella said, dabbing her eyes with the hem of her blouse. "I'm trying to stay calm. Anyway, I poked my head into the mill and saw nothing, so I stepped inside. There's a storeroom off the main room, and I suddenly heard footsteps scuttling around in it. Whoever was there cleared his throat—I could tell it was a man. I was about to call out to Mr. Isaacs—but just then I had a feeling it wasn't him. I noticed part of a corner wall had been knocked out. I figured that was the noise I had heard."

Rafaella's voice started to quiver as she struggled to finish her story. Then she leaned her head on Nancy's shoulder and began to cry.

"Don't worry, Rafaella," Nancy said soothingly, "everything's okay now. I just need to hear the rest of your story so we can try to catch this person."

"Yes, I know," Rafaella sobbed as tears streamed down her cheeks. "It's just so awful."

"I know," Nancy said patiently. "But the bad stuff is over now. Can you tell me what happened next?"

Rafaella sat up and squared her shoulders as she fought back her tears. After a few moments her voice was steady enough to speak. "Whoever attacked me must have climbed out a window in the storeroom, run around the mill, and come in through the door behind me to knock me out," she told Nancy. "The next thing I knew, I was tied to the pole with the ants crawling toward me. I tried to scream for help, but I couldn't." Her doelike eyes searched Nancy's face. "What if you hadn't found me?"

"But I did," Nancy said calmly. "And you're okay." Nancy stood up. "I'd like to search the mill for clues. Will you be all right out here for a moment?"

Rafaella nodded anxiously. "I think I'll be okay, Nancy, but hurry."

"I will," Nancy promised.

She stepped into the mill. Carefully avoiding the teeming ants in the piles of sugar, Nancy poked around the room, scouting for anything, no matter how small, that the person might have left behind. Much of the wood in the mill was rotten, and Nancy's foot almost broke through the floorboards twice. Cobwebs hung from the huge machinery that had ground up the sugar so many years ago.

Remembering Rafaella's description of a corner wall being knocked out, Nancy gingerly walked over the broken floor to the nearest corner. Sure enough, some pieces of each intersecting wall were missing with fresh breaks in the wood.

Taking care as she walked, Nancy examined the three other corners. A number of boards were missing there, too, she observed, but the breaks looked a few days old. Nancy ran her fingers over the jagged edges of the splintered wood. This person was really determined, she thought, eyeing the hacked-up walls. He must have been working on this place for the past few days.

A sudden thought struck Nancy—the person must not have found the necklace yet, or else he wouldn't have still been working on the walls. Unless, Nancy realized, he'd found it just before Rafaella surprised him.

Nancy's mind clicked away. One of the clues in

Miranda's letter must refer to the corners of the old mill. Judging from the attacker's desperate hacking, Nancy bet the necklace was still where Miranda had hidden it.

Moving into the storeroom, Nancy searched more. Floorboards creaked ominously under her body weight. Her skin prickled—if several boards fell through at once, she would plummet into the rushing creek below her.

The window on her right was an open square with no panes or casement. Looking through it, Nancy decided that Rafaella's attacker must have climbed out and then skirted the mill to hit Rafaella from behind.

Hazy sunlight filtered through dust motes as Nancy studied the old wooden bins in the room. She peered inside the first one. It was empty, but she guessed that long ago these bins had been used to store sugar.

She opened the next bin, which was deeper than the first. The light was dim at the bottom, but a faint square of white caught her eye. Reaching inside, she picked it up.

It was a book of matches, with words printed on one side. Closing the lid to the sugar bin, Nancy studied the inscription. The words *L'Hotel Eaton* were dashed in bold red script across the front. An address in Paris appeared underneath in black print.

Nancy frowned as she considered the clue. Pierre was from Paris, and Eaton was the name of the family who had owned the famous emerald.

Nancy stared at the matchbook, thinking. Could Pierre have something to do with the Eatons? she wondered.

14

Boating Toward Disaster

Nancy put the matchbook in the pocket of her cut-off jeans. Then she reached back into the bin, sweeping her hand over the bottom to see if anything else might have been dropped. Whoever attacked Rafaella may have tried to hide in the bin before realizing he might get caught there, she reasoned.

This time, the bin was empty. After shutting the lid, Nancy went back to Rafaella.

"Are you ready to go, Nancy?" Rafaella asked hopefully. "I sure hope we catch this person."

"Me, too," Nancy said. As they walked back to the house, Nancy asked, "By the way, Rafaella, you *did* lose an earring. The owner of the jewelry store told me you'd come back to buy another pair. So why did you tell me you hadn't?"

Rafaella blushed. "I didn't want anyone to know I'd been in Mr. and Mrs. Isaacs's bedroom. Promise you won't tell, Nancy?"

"I promise," Nancy said, "but why were you there?"

"It was just before you arrived from the airport. Mrs. Isaacs had gone upstairs to take a nap after lunch, and she asked me to wake her by three to greet you. But when I went upstairs, the room was empty—she'd already gotten up.

"Just then I noticed some pictures on Mrs. Isaacs's bureau of her and Mr. Isaacs. I thought they were lovely, so I bent forward to see them better. My earring caught on a lamp, and the feather broke off, but I didn't have a chance to pick it up because I suddenly heard the Isaacses in the downstairs hall. I had to beat a hasty retreat, or they would have thought I was snooping in their room."

"What about the lemonade glass?" Nancy asked. "Was that yours?"

Rafaella tucked her chin down, looking guilty. "I feel awful—I never should have taken it upstairs. I put it on Mrs. Isaacs's bureau to look at the pictures, and I spilled it when I heard Mr. and Mrs. Isaacs. I was startled, you see, and I knocked against the bureau. I didn't have a chance to clean it up."

"Thanks for telling me, Rafaella," Nancy said. "And don't worry—I won't tell anyone."

Back at the house, the Isaacses were drinking orange juice on the veranda. Nancy told them what had happened to Rafaella.

Emma rushed over to Rafaella. "You poor thing!" she cried. "Are you sure you're all right? I don't think you ought to make breakfast for us today, Rafaella. I think you should go to your room, take a long shower, and rest. We can take care of ourselves."

Rafaella smiled in relief. "Thanks, Mrs. Isaacs. I think I'll take you up on your suggestion. But please don't worry—you can expect dinner as usual."

Rising from his chair, Jack thanked Rafaella. As she left the porch, Jack faced the others and said, "We've got to call in Sam McClain. This business here at Sugar Moon has reached a dangerous point. It would be irresponsible not to tell the sheriff."

Nancy frowned. She wanted to do more investigating on her own before the police were involved. If the intruder noticed police at Sugar Moon, he might panic and destroy the rest of Miranda's letter with the last three clues. After all, that page could be evidence against him if anyone found it.

Nancy told the Isaacses her thoughts. Jack frowned, then said, "All right, Nancy, we'll give you one more day to find this person. But please be careful. Your safety is much more important than a letter or a necklace."

"I promise I'll be careful, Jack. Why don't I fix some breakfast for us?" Nancy offered. "Emma, would you mind showing me how to light your oven? I thought I'd warm up some muffins."

"Sure thing, Nancy," Emma said eagerly.

Nancy smiled to herself—she'd hoped to get a moment alone with Emma. She wanted to settle the question of Old Ironbones once and for all.

In the kitchen Nancy said, "Emma, if I'm going to get to the bottom of what's going on at Sugar Moon, I need to know about you and Old Ironbones."

Emma paled and shook her head.

"I know you met him on the beach and went into the woods with him," Nancy went on. "Ned and I saw you. What did you hand him, anyway?"

Emma's freckled nose tilted upward as she fixed Nancy with a challenging stare. But Nancy refused to look away. Finally Emma dropped her gaze. "You can't tell Jack this," she began in a resigned tone.

She stole a glance over her shoulder as if making sure they were alone, then turned back to Nancy and whispered, "I give Old Ironbones money to feed his stray pets. But Jack doesn't approve."

"Don't worry, Emma, I won't tell," Nancy assured her.

In a low voice Emma explained, "On the morning

of our cocktail party, I agreed to give Old Ironbones some cash for his animals if we met at noon. But he never showed up. Instead, he came for the money during our party and caused a scene when Jack asked him to come back another time. Jack likes animals, but he's allergic to most of them. He's not passionate about them the way I am, and he doesn't like me to indulge Old Ironbones because the old man is undependable and kooky. But I gave him the money anyway the night that you and Ned spotted us."

"But why are you so sure Old Ironbones hasn't been snooping around Sugar Moon?" Nancy asked.

"Because I know him. I see the gentle way he handles his pets. I admit he's not great with people, and it was upsetting when he threatened us on your first day here. But he's nothing more than a crazy old tramp. He's not organized enough to plan a search through someone's house, much less sneak poison onto a salad in a crowded restaurant."

Privately, Nancy thought that Emma was excusing the old man's excitable behavior too easily, but she agreed that he probably wasn't the thief.

As Emma and Nancy took trays of muffins, coffee, and fruit out to the veranda, Nancy caught sight of several pieces of furniture assembled in the front hall. "What are those?" she asked, taking a detour through the dining room and into the front hall.

Following her, Emma replied, "Duncan Adams's

auction is today, so Jack and I thought we'd get rid of some of our stuff. Otherwise, we'll have to wait till next month, and we need cash for house repairs. We brought the pieces down early this morning while you were at the mill."

Nancy set her tray down on a side table while she went to inspect the furniture. One of the items was an old chest of drawers with a crusty, water-stained surface. The initials MJ were engraved on a small brass plaque on the top.

Nancy looked at Emma. "MJ—this could be Miranda's chest!"

"According to Duncan, it is," Emma answered. "It has sentimental value, I know, but the wood in the back is rotting and we can't use it. For some reason, old Mr. Jenkins stashed it away in the basement for years, and this damp tropical climate has given it wormwood. But Duncan thinks we'll still get good money for it—enough people on the island know Miranda's history and would collect it for that reason alone."

Emma checked her watch. "Uh, oh, Nancy—it's already eight-thirty, and I told Duncan I'd have the furniture to him by nine for a last-minute display. He usually asks for stuff a week ahead, but he was kind enough to give us a break today. Jack and I won't have time for breakfast, but you eat. The auction starts at eleven."

"Let me go through the drawers first," Nancy asked. She quickly checked them but they were empty. On a nearby table, she saw a small porcelain piggy bank shaped like a well. Miranda's wishing well? Nancy wondered.

She picked it up and inspected it. On the bottom was written: "Miranda, you are all I could ever wish for, Giles." Eagerly, Nancy shook it, hoping to hear the necklace rattling inside. But no such luck. She sighed, putting it down. The real clue *must* be on the page that's still missing!

Nancy asked Emma if she could use her phone to call long distance, Emma agreed, and while the Isaacs moved the furniture into Emma's pickup truck, Nancy fished the matchbook from her pocket and dialed L'Hotel Eaton from the front hall.

A woman's voice answered. "Is this Mrs. Eaton?" Nancy asked her in French.

"Yes," the woman answered. "May I help you?" Despite the woman's fluent French, Nancy recognized an American accent. She switched to English.

"I'd like to speak to Pierre Lavaud," Nancy fudged. "Is he there? This is a college friend of his, but we've been out of touch lately."

"Pierre?" the woman said. "I'm sorry. He's spending the year in the Caribbean. Would you like his number? This is his mother."

"Oh, but didn't you say your name is Eaton?" Nancy asked.

The woman gave a soft laugh. "After Pierre's father and I were divorced, I took back my maiden name. Then I started this hotel and named it after my American family."

"I see," Nancy said. After pretending to take down Pierre's number, Nancy thanked her and hung up.

"Just what do you think you're doing?" a familiar voice asked at her shoulder.

Nancy whirled around to find Bess scowling at her.

"If you're trying to dig up dirt on Pierre," Bess said indignantly, "don't bother. I can vouch for him, Nancy. I mean, I wasn't so sure after he left me with the barracuda, but when we danced together last night, I just *know* he's innocent."

Nancy laughed. "Bess, how can one night of dancing make you so sure?"

At that moment Ned joined them, sleepily running a hand through his dark brown hair.

"Ned, Bess," Nancy said eagerly, "listen to this." Quickly she updated them on the case.

"So Rafaella and Old Ironbones are out of the picture," Ned said. "And Duncan, too."

"But it's *got* to be Duncan," Bess protested. "After all, he's greedy for stuff to sell at his auction."

"But how do you explain the matchbook?" Ned asked.

Bess's eyes clouded over. "Pierre could have dropped it some other time," she muttered.

"I want to search Pierre's boat for the missing page," Nancy said. "If it's not there, maybe we can sneak into his house. Will you guys help me?"

"Absolutely," Ned replied. "Let's get going. We can always eat later."

Bess pursed her lips. "You're wasting your time with Pierre. I'll just spend the morning sunbathing." She flounced off to grab a muffin, then headed out to the front porch.

"See you later, Bess," Nancy called out. "Alert the police if we don't come back!"

Bess promised to keep track of the time they were gone, and Nancy and Ned hurried out the door. Soon, they were jogging down the path that led by the old sugar mill. After passing the mill, they continued until the path opened on to a small beach where a boat was moored to a dock. A boxlike house sat upon a bluff above.

"Pierre's boat," Nancy whispered, "and it looks as if no one's around. Let's sneak closer."

"I'm going to check out the house to make sure we're really alone," Ned suggested. "We wouldn't want him to be up there watching us."

"Good idea, Ned."

Ned squeezed her hand and added, "Good luck, Nan. Shout if you need me." Then he hurried up the stone steps to the house.

Scanning the beach, Nancy moved silently toward Pierre's boat. A light breeze whispered through a nearby grove of palms. Tiny waves slapped gently against the boat's hull. Otherwise, everything was quiet.

Nancy climbed on to the boat. Peering down the steps that led into the cabin, Nancy felt her pulse race. What if Pierre was in there?

Like a cat creeping toward a mouse, Nancy stepped down to the cabin noiselessly. Her heart pounded hard in her chest as she peeked into the tiny room. To her relief, it was empty.

Nancy made a beeline for Pierre's desk. She didn't want to waste a second. Pierre could come back any time.

After checking several drawers above his blotter and finding nothing but pencils and stationery, Nancy tried a drawer to the right of the desk. It was locked.

Nancy took off her barrette. Her reddish blond hair swung around her shoulders as she pried open the lock with the metal prong. Seconds later the drawer sprang open.

A thrill went through Nancy as she stared at the open drawer. At the front lay a folded piece of paper, yellow with age. The missing page of Miranda's letter!

Nancy's hands shook with excitement as she unfolded the paper. Sure enough, the clues continued where they had left off. Nancy read quickly, beguiled once more by Miranda's romantic voice:

4) Inside my diary where I write only of you.
5) In the corner of the sugar mill where our initials are carved. 6) My heart beats for you in my chest's secret place.

Darling Giles, I hope they'll free you soon. The E.E. belongs to you now. One of these clues will find it for you. Treasure it in my memory, always. May God be with you.

The page ended, but Nancy knew that the rest of the letter contained only Miranda's closing and her signature.

So Miranda did mention the E.E. on this page, Nancy observed. Obviously, Pierre had guessed what it was.

Nancy studied the clues. Probably clue number five was a red herring, she thought, remembering the hacked-up corners of the mill where Pierre had been frantically working. But what about the diary? Pierre must have been looking for it in the attic at Sugar Moon, as well as for the first part of the letter.

Casting her mind back to the boxes in the attic, Nancy couldn't think of anything that resembled a diary. It could be lost, she mused.

Nancy zeroed in on the sixth clue. Her mind flashed to the chest of drawers in the Isaacses' hall. Could "my chest" refer to Miranda's bureau that Emma and Jack are selling? she wondered. Maybe there was a secret compartment in it.

Nancy chewed her lip. Of all six clues, a secret drawer in a chest would be the best hiding place for a necklace. And it would be easy for Miranda, in her weakened condition, to hide it there.

Nancy's heart fluttered with excitement as she thought about the chest. Pierre probably hasn't clued into it yet, she thought. After all, he'd been hacking away at the mill as of this morning, which meant he hadn't found the necklace. There was no evidence he'd been near the chest since then.

It was ten o'clock, Nancy saw, checking her watch. The chest will be auctioned at eleven. I've got to get over to Hidden Treasure to stop the auction.

A revving sound suddenly filled the air. Nancy whirled around. She ran for the companionway. She was only halfway up when the boat took off with a roar.

She glimpsed a dark-haired man leap off the deck and on to the dock. Pierre!

The boat swerved as it careened, unguided,

through the water, speeding along the shore. Nancy was slammed against the wall.

On the dock, Pierre laughed wildly as he watched Nancy, now on deck, struggle toward the wheel. The violent motion of the boat was tossing her every which way. Gritting her teeth, Nancy lurched forward, desperate to control her flailing arms and legs. She had to reach the helm before the boat crashed!

15

A Bid Against Evil

Should I jump? Nancy wondered, peering over the rail.

The water churned white around the sides of the boat. Huge waves rose up in its wake. No way, she decided—the boat is going too fast, and I could get caught in the propeller.

Just then several small black specks appeared about a hundred yards in front of the boat. Nancy felt a rush of horror—it was a group of swimmers, and if she didn't act soon, they'd be run over by the boat!

Nancy forced herself toward the wheel. The boat zigzagged through the water, threatening to toss her overboard.

I'm almost there, she kept telling herself. I've got to grab the helm so I can steer.

With one last effort of will, Nancy threw herself forward—and touched the helm.

It shuddered under her hands, but she gripped it hard to steady the boat. Just before the boat reached the swimmers, Nancy swerved, missing one man by only a couple of feet.

Adrenaline pumped through her as she steadied the boat, turning it to head in a straight line out to sea. She was still going way too fast. Studying the control panel, Nancy recognized the throttle. She pushed it in. Immediately, the boat slowed. Finally! Nancy breathed deeply.

With the boat under control, Nancy turned it back to shore and Pierre's dock.

I wonder how Ned is, she thought anxiously. I hope Pierre didn't catch him in the house and hurt him.

As Nancy approached the dock, she saw a dark-haired guy lying motionless on the beach. Her mouth went dry. Could that be Ned? She drew closer.

"Hey, Nancy!" a familiar voice called out. Nancy's heart fluttered with relief as she saw Ned jogging toward her from the woods near the house. "Are you okay?" he asked. "I was just on my way to Sugar Moon to phone for help."

She smiled as she brought the boat alongside the dock. "I'm fine, Ned, thanks. And I'm glad to see that you're okay, too." She nodded toward Pierre. "For a moment I got worried. I thought he might be you."

Ned wrinkled his brow. "We might look a little alike, Nan," he said doubtfully, "but you have to admit our personalities are pretty different."

"Are they?" Nancy teased, smiling at him fondly.

Ned grinned, then helped her secure the line to the dock. Once it was tied, they walked over to Pierre, who was out cold.

Nancy stooped down and saw that he was breathing evenly. He stirred for a moment and mumbled something. "I think he's about to come to, but we should probably call a doctor just to make sure he's okay," Nancy said. She glanced at Ned curiously. "What did you do to him, anyway?"

"I didn't realize how hard I punched him," Ned replied ruefully. "The minute I saw him casting you out to sea, I rushed down from the house to help you. Pierre tackled me. I was so angry at him, I didn't realize my own strength. But if I hadn't hit him first, he would have knocked me out, for sure."

Nancy quickly told Ned about finding the rest of Miranda's letter, and also her hunch about the chest.

"Then let's not waste another minute!" Ned urged. "But before we go to the auction, we'll call a doctor from Sugar Moon. Pierre's house is locked. I found that out when I was checking to see if someone was around."

After pulling Pierre above the high tide mark, Nancy and Ned sprinted back down the trail to Sugar Moon. Once there, they burst into the house and called emergency paramedics to help Pierre.

Just as Nancy was hanging up, Rafaella timidly poked her face around the doorjamb between the dining room and the hall. "Whew—it's you," Rafaella said in a tone of relief. Then she boldly joined Nancy and Ned in the hall. "Whenever I hear a strange noise, I get jumpy," she explained.

"No wonder, after what you went through in the sugar mill," Ned said.

"Rafaella, have you seen Bess?" Nancy asked.

"She went with Mr. and Mrs. Isaacs to the auction," Rafaella replied.

Nancy checked her watch. It was already eleven—the auction was about to begin. "Would you do us a huge favor?" she asked. "We need to get over to the auction right away. Could you drive us there?"

Rafaella smiled. "That's a small favor to ask after what you did for me, Nancy," she said. "Let's go."

They all climbed into Rafaella's pickup truck and started down the long driveway to the road. Nancy's fingernails dug into her palms as she thought about Miranda's chest. What if it has already been sold?

They bounced into town, avoiding the stray goats, dogs, and chickens that casually roamed the roads. Rafaella zoomed down the final stretch to the center of town, then ground to a halt in front of Hidden Treasure. The drone of voices reverberated from a warehouse next door.

After thanking Rafaella, Nancy and Ned hopped out of the truck. Nancy glanced at her watch as she yanked open the warehouse door. It was eleven-fifteen.

Inside, rows of chairs with two side aisles filled a cavernous space. Most of the seats were taken.

At the front of the room, Duncan Adams stood at the podium, gleefully pounding his gavel. Behind him was a mass of furniture, paintings, and bric-a-brac.

"Sold for six hundred dollars," he bellowed, "to the lady in the red hat." He jabbed a thick finger toward an older woman in the back row.

"Oh no!" Nancy groaned. "I hope he didn't just sell Miranda's chest."

At that moment a young man—Duncan's assistant, Nancy assumed—scurried up to the woman, bearing a framed engraving of an exotic-looking shore bird.

"Not yet, I guess," Ned whispered as the woman propped the picture against the chair in front of her.

"I've got to ask Duncan to let me search Miranda's chest before he puts it up for auction," Nancy said. She started down the nearest aisle toward the podium. But just as she reached the middle of the aisle, two assistants carried a chest of drawers forward and set it next to Duncan. Nancy's heart skipped a beat—it was Miranda's!

Duncan puffed out his chest proudly. "We have here a beautiful Victorian chest of drawers," he announced. "It once belonged to a famous local beauty, Miranda Jenkins. Her initials are engraved in brass on the top. Who would like to start the bidding at five hundred dollars? Do I hear five hundred?"

Nancy opened her mouth to stop the sale, when Duncan yelled, "Five hundred dollars from the gentleman over there." He pointed to a man in the far corner who had already raised his hand. "Do I hear five fifty?" he went on.

Oh no! Nancy thought, horrified. This auction is happening way too fast. I can't stop someone from buying that chest if he's already made a bid.

For a split second, Nancy felt paralyzed. Then

she made a decision. She took a deep breath and prayed that her hunch about the necklace was right.

"Do I hear five fifty?" Duncan repeated.

Nancy raised her hand.

"We have five fifty, ladies and gentlemen, from the young lady standing in the aisle," Duncan proclaimed.

From several rows ahead, Nancy spotted Bess and the Isaacses looking back at her as if she'd lost her mind.

"Do I hear six hundred?" Duncan shouted. The man in the corner raised his hand. With a joyful grin, Duncan said, "We have six hundred from the gentleman over there. Do I hear six fifty?"

Once more Nancy raised her hand.

"Six hundred and fifty it is, from the young lady," Duncan cried happily. "Do I hear seven?"

The man raised his hand.

"Seven hundred it is," Duncan said. "Do I hear seven fifty?"

"One thousand," a voice behind Nancy shouted.

Nancy turned. Her heart sank at the sight of Pierre standing behind her, raising his hand for the bid. His left eye was swollen and he looked a little pale, but his eyes glinted with steely determination.

"One thousand dollars it is," Duncan yelled, "to the gentleman standing in the aisle."

Nancy swallowed. "Twelve hundred!" she cried.

Pierre fixed her with a challenging stare. "Fifteen hundred!" he exclaimed.

"Fifteen hundred dollars from the gentleman in the aisle," Duncan announced. "Do I hear sixteen hundred?"

Nancy hesitated. The bids were getting very expensive, and there was a chance the chest might not hide the necklace at all. Could she really take that kind of a risk?

Nancy caught Jack's eye as he craned around toward Pierre. She pointed frantically at the chest and mouthed *necklace*.

"Do I hear sixteen hundred?" Duncan repeated.

Jack whispered something to a man on his left. As Jack spoke, the man looked from Pierre to Nancy to the chest. Then he stood up. Nancy recognized Sam McClain, the sheriff of Saint Ann.

"Going for fifteen hundred," Duncan announced. He raised his gavel. "Going, going—"

"Wait a minute, folks. Hold the auction right there!" the sheriff announced, weaving his way toward the aisle.

With his gavel suspended in midair, Duncan gaped at Sam as he strode up to the chest.

"I'm sorry to say that this chest of drawers has been confiscated in the name of the law," the sheriff said, placing a hand on it.

"Just what is the meaning of this?" Duncan sputtered, bringing down his gavel on the podium with a bang. "What do you think you're doing, Sam McClain?"

The sheriff pointed at Pierre. "I'd like to detain this young man for questioning," he said. Turning to Nancy, he added, "And I'd like this young lady to check out this beautiful chest."

Nancy flashed him a grateful smile and stepped up to the chest. The necklace had better be here, she thought, opening the top right drawer. She tried not to feel the audience's eyes upon her as she tapped the wood for a hollow panel.

"Nothing," she murmured to herself in disappointment.

Sam led Pierre forward while Nancy opened the top left drawer. She tapped the sides hopefully. When she came to the back panel, she hesitated. There's a button there, I know it, she thought, feeling a slight knob in the wood.

Nancy pressed it—and held her breath. Sure enough, to her complete delight, a small secret drawer sprang out of the panel. In the center was a crinkly old envelope with *Giles* written on it in Miranda's elegant script.

As the audience began to crowd around her, Nancy tore open the envelope. Reaching inside, she drew out the most gorgeous necklace she'd ever

141

seen. Nine emeralds the color of summer leaves gleamed on a strand of platinum. The largest emerald, about an inch in diameter, hung in the center like a tear. It was encased in a setting of diamonds and tiny pearls.

A hush went through the room as everyone stared at the necklace. Nancy handed it to Sam McClain. Then she reached into the envelope again and took out a note.

" 'Darling Giles,' " she read to the crowd, " 'You have found my heart. Miranda.' "

Nancy folded the note and sighed. Despite her excitement at finding the necklace, she felt a twinge of sadness. Obviously, Giles had never read Miranda's note nor found the necklace. She must have died before she had had the chance to send him the letter. Turning to Duncan, Nancy asked, "Whatever happened to Giles, anyway?"

Duncan looked stunned as he stared at the necklace in Sam McClain's hand. "I . . . I can't believe it, you found her necklace," he muttered. "So the legend really was based on fact—Giles did give the necklace to her."

Duncan rubbed his forehead, as if he were willing himself back to the present. "Excuse me, what did you ask me, Miss Drew?"

Nancy repeated her question.

"Ah yes," Duncan went on. "Giles Wentworth escaped from prison after a year. He was killed in a duel in Jamaica shortly after that."

Bess turned to the sheriff and asked, "What's going to happen to the necklace now?"

"I'm going to track down the descendants of the original Mrs. Eaton," he told her. "After all, it belongs to them."

Pierre shifted uncomfortably on his feet as the sheriff mentioned the Eatons.

Bess took Nancy aside. In a worried tone, she whispered, "But don't these descendants include Pierre?"

"I guess so," Nancy said. "I'm not sure that Sheriff McClain realizes Pierre is an Eaton. Of course, Pierre could go to jail for attempted murder, so the necklace won't do him much good there."

"Well, he should go to jail," Bess said indignantly.

Nancy grinned. "Bess Marvin! You kept sticking up for him."

"Don't remind me," Bess said, rolling her eyes. "I must have gone temporarily crazy. But you've got to admit, Nan, that he seemed nice."

Just then Duncan pounded his gavel and announced that the auction would continue. While the audience took their seats, Sam led Pierre out the front door and motioned for the girls, Ned, and the Isaacses to follow.

Once outside, he turned to the group and asked,

"Does anyone have questions for this young man before I take him down to the station for official interrogation?"

"I do," Nancy said. Looking Pierre in the eye, she asked, "How did you know to show up at the auction? Did you suddenly guess the sixth clue?"

"I used a better method than guesswork," Pierre said smugly. "When you and Ned were talking by the dock, I was actually conscious. But I pretended not to be so I could overhear your conversation."

"So by the time the paramedics got there, you were gone," Ned said.

"You bet," Pierre answered.

"You might as well admit to being the intruder at Sugar Moon," Jack declared. "Why else would you be so interested in bidding on the chest, if you hadn't been snooping around our attic looking for it in the first place?"

Pierre hung his head. Reluctantly, he said, "Yes, I was the intruder. I came across part of Miranda's letter by chance while I was helping you work, Jack. And, yes, I hit Nancy on the head in the attic. That's why I put the poison on her salad—I thought she'd seen me there."

"You were lucky to be able to sneak on the poison without being seen at the Flying Fish," Nancy told him.

"Ah—but I'm good at being sneaky, Nancy," Pierre said proudly. "I was checking in the evening at the Scuba Shop to see when I had to work when I noticed you entering the Flying Fish. I'd picked some manchineel fruit earlier at Pirate's Rock, in case I'd get an opportunity to put it on your food later. I saw my chance."

"So you left us with those barracuda on purpose, Pierre?" Bess asked in a hurt tone.

Pierre chuckled. "I thought I'd give you guys a little scare, even though I knew they probably wouldn't hurt you. And just for the record, I tied Rafaella in the sugar mill because I was worried that she'd seen me, and I sneaked the last page of the letter into Ned's pocket as a warning to Nancy."

As Sheriff McClain led him away, he turned back toward Nancy and snarled, "Too bad my warning didn't work."

"This sure is the life, guys," Bess said, basking in the sunlight on board a fishing boat in the Saint Ann harbor. "Maybe we'll even catch a couple of barracuda."

It was the day after the auction, and Bess, Nancy, and Ned were about to set off for a half day's fishing trip. At that moment Sam McClain approached the boat, wearing his white pith helmet.

"Hi there, kids," he said. "I thought you might be interested in what I found out about the Eatons."

"Definitely," Ned told him, leaning forward.

"Pierre's branch of the Eatons descended from Mr. Felix Eaton's brother," Sam explained. "So Pierre had no right to the necklace, but since its theft was well known in the family, Pierre must have realized exactly what Miranda meant by the E.E. when he discovered the clues in her letter. He took a big interest in the necklace—for personal reasons as well as for greed."

"Hmm. I think the greed part did this," Nancy said dryly, fingering the bruise on her head.

The sheriff shot Nancy a grateful look. "Thank you so much, Nancy—and Ned and Bess, too—for all your help in solving this case. Nancy, your quick thinking broke Miranda's code in the nick of time."

Bess cocked her head. "So who gets the necklace?" she asked him.

"Mrs. Felix Eaton's great-great-granddaughter," Sam answered. "She's an old lady who lives in New York City. Years ago she gave all her money and possessions away to charity, but she'll treasure the necklace as a memento. When her granddaughter turns twenty-one, she'll inherit it."

"Along with its romantic history," Bess gushed.

"Just tell her not to take it to the Caribbean," Ned quipped.

After Sam waved good-bye, Nancy turned to her friends and said, "Well, guys, how about some fishing?"

Ned grinned, putting an arm around Nancy's shoulders. "As long as it's fish you're planning to catch, Nan, and not another mystery."

The most puzzling mysteries...
The cleverest crimes...
The most dynamic
brother detectives!

The Hardy Boys®

By Franklin W. Dixon

Join Frank and Joe Hardy in up-to-date
adventures packed with action and suspense

Look for brand-new mysteries
wherever books are sold

Available from Minstrel® Books
Published by Pocket Books

2314

**The Fascinating Story of
One of the World's Most
Celebrated Naturalists**

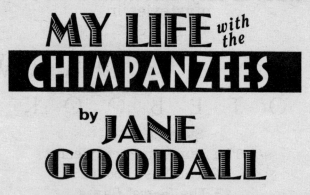

MY LIFE with the CHIMPANZEES

by JANE GOODALL

From the time she was girl, Jane Goodall dreamed
of a life spent working with animals. Finally, when she
was twenty-six years old, she ventured into the forests
of Africa to observe chimpanzees in the wild. On her
expeditions she braved the dangers of the jungle
and survived encounters with leopards and lions
in the African bush. And she got to know an amazing
group of wild chimpanzees—intelligent animals whose
lives bear a surprising resemblance to our own.

Illustrated with photographs

A Byron Preiss Visual Publications, Inc. Book

**A Minstrel® Book
Published by Pocket Books**

2403